THE BIG BOOK OF KIDS' GAMES

Tracy Stephen Burroughs

Longmeadow Press

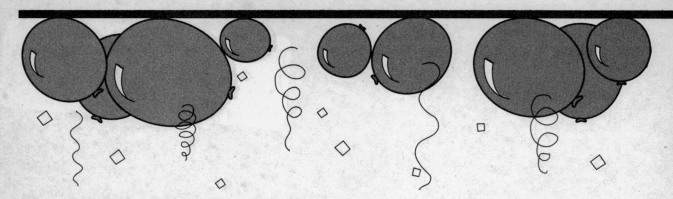

All of the activities in this book should be prepared and organized with complete parental supervision.

Cover design by Frank Stinga
Interior design by Allan Mogel
Illustrated by Tracy Stephen Borroughs

Library of Congress Cataloging-in-Publication Data

Burroughs, Tracy Stephen.
    The big book of kid's games : ages 8–15 / by Tracy Stephen Burroughs.
        p.   cm.
    Summary: Presents a collection of wet and messy party games to be played indoors and outdoors using common household or easily found materials.
    ISBN 0-681-41456-1:
    1. Games—Juvenile literature. [1. Games.]
I. Title.
GV1203.B79   1992
790.1'922—dc20   91-36495
                                        CIP
                                        AC

Printed in United States of America
First Edition

        0 9 8 7 6 5 4 3 2 1

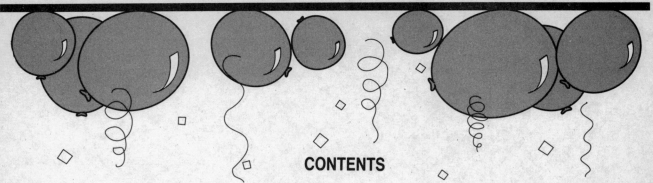

CONTENTS

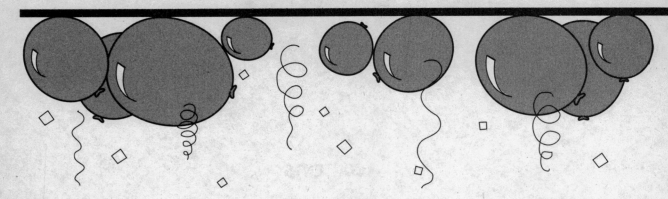

Introduction

Welcome to the "slime-me" generation. On some of the shows I write for—*Family Double Dare, Think Fast, Get the Picture, Make the Grade* and *Total Panic*—kids compete against each other in outrageously fun games and sometimes get doused in chocolate sauce, drenched with Jell-O and sloshed with whipped cream. Using common household and easily found materials you can recreate the same challenges. This book is dedicated to kids that like those games (and the ones that like indoor, outdoor, dry and brainy ones too) and the parents, schools, and community groups that want to organize fantastically fun events for parties, fairs, and social events for kids eight to fifteen years old.

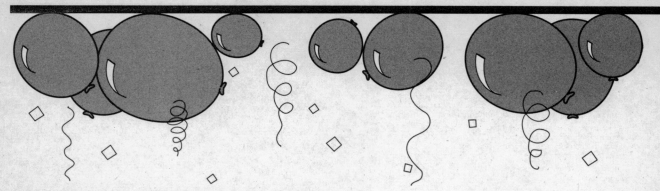

Important Things to Consider:

1. Have all the players wear sneakers.

2. All the games should be played under the supervision of an adult, who can also act as the referee when needed.

3. For most games, I have suggested time limits but this, of course, depends on the kids playing the game. If, while the game is in progress, you find it is more difficult for the players than you thought, then add on thirty seconds, or one or two minutes more, and make an announcement that you're doing so. If the challenge seems too easy, then shorten the game. For all games that depend on time limits, periodically let the players know how much time is left.

4. Keep in mind that many games designated as "indoors" can be played outdoors, and vice versa, if you make a few adjustments.

5. You might want to give kids a choice of which games they want to play before the party.

6. How old are the children participating? Can that age level play the game effectively? If you are not sure about how well a game will work, try it out in advance.

7. To add more fun to your event, give names to the teams, or have them invent their own. Of course, the crazier the better: "The Slimes," "Turtle Power," "Ultimate Champion," "Awesome Dudes and Dudettes," "Narly Creations from Outer Space."

8. For many of these games, teams can compete at the same time. This is usually more fun than having one team complete a game before the competing team starts, but of course, sometimes this isn't possible.

9. Always keep kids occupied. If you're planning several games, have them all set up and ready to go so they can be done one after another.

10. When setting up a game, make sure that all the variables involved are equal for each team or player.

11. If you put tape on the floor to mark off starting points and finish lines, make sure it's the kind that can be easily removed when the games are over. Or, draw a chalk line, which can be wiped off with a damp sponge.

12. For games that involve wet materials like water, whipped cream, shaving cream, and Jell-O, you should keep a mop on hand and lay a thin painter's plastic drop cloth on the floor for easy cleanup. You might consider having a couple of drop cloths for use between consecutive messy games. (These can be bought in a paint shop or a hardware store.) As the surface may get slippery, have adults or older children act as spotters, ready to catch anyone who might fall.

13. Don't use materials that will stain. Some kids may feel self-conscious at first about getting dirty or messy, but soon they will be caught up in the exhilaration and fun of it all.

14. For wet games a change of clothing is recommended, or you can provide inexpensive paper painter's jump suits, full-length rain jackets, or even extra-long plastic garbage bags with holes cut out for heads and arms. Also, have towels ready for quick cleanup.

15. Many of the games involve food. If you would rather not be wasteful, substitute something else like water, sand, or styrofoam packaging peanuts. Use your imagination: Just make sure it's appropriate for the game. Also, if several buckets are needed, buy very inexpensive cardboard painter's buckets at paint or hardware stores. For bowls use disposable tin-foil baking pans, and get small cardboard boxes for dry materials.

16. If you play games for prizes, we suggest giving a little something to all the participants just for being good sports, even if it's candy or a small prize.

17. Finally, remind the children that it doesn't really matter who wins, because we're here to have fun!

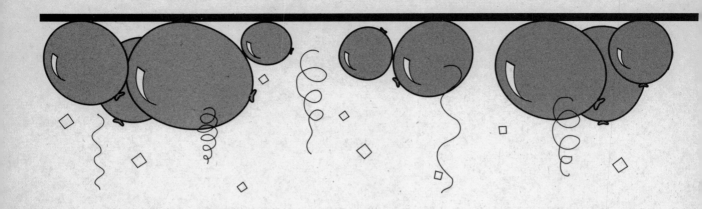

Indoor
or
Outdoor
Games

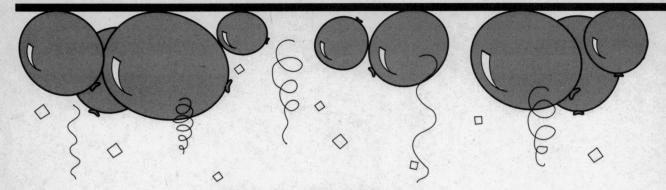

Pop-A-Thon

Materials for Each Player: 6 balloons.

Players: Teams of 2 or more players each or individuals playing against each other.

How It's Played: Each team has before them an equal number of water balloons. At the starting sound they have to stomp on them in their bare feet and break them as fast as they can. The team that breaks all their balloons first wins. Give each team their own color balloon so it will be easier to keep score.

Yucky Stuff

Materials Needed: Poster board, markers, ten boxes (each about one-foot square), and an assortment of objects, toys, or food. (Use your imagination.)

Players: Individuals play against each other, or have teams of 3 or more players each.

How It's Played: Cut 2 sets of holes in the sides of your boxes, so 2 players at a time can stick their hands in. Place a different toy, object, or food in each box. Examples of foods are grapes, Jell-O, sugar, wet pasta, and egg yolks. (Wet stuff is more fun.)

At the starting sound, 2 teams at a time go down the row of boxes, one team on each side, and stick their hands in to feel what's inside. Then the captains of the teams secretly confer with their teammates and write down on the pieces of poster board, *in order*, what was in the boxes. (Spelling doesn't count.) At any time, players can go back to the boxes to get a second feel. When all the teams are ready, their answers are taped to the wall.

The team with the most correct answers wins. those not participating can get a list of the answers in advance so they are in on the fun.

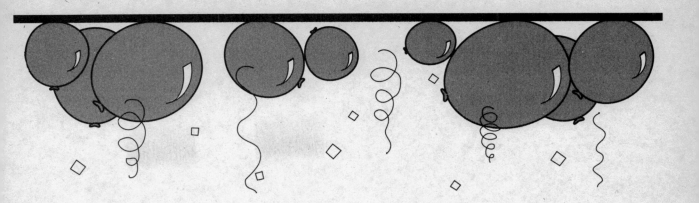

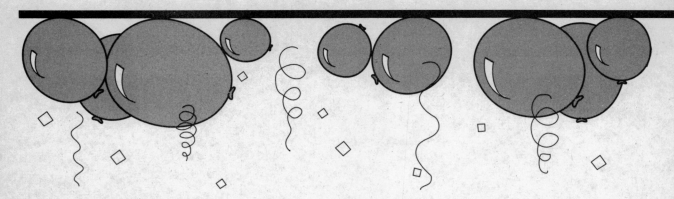

The Switcheroo Challenge

Materials for Each Player: A shoe box or small corrugated cardboard box, a 3 foot length of yarn or string, and 2 golfballs the same color. (If only white balls are available, they can be marked with different colored markers.)

Players: Teams of 2 or 4 players each.

How It's Played: The players wear boxes strapped to their chests, which have 2 balls the same color inside. (See diagram below.) For each team, 2 sets of different colored balls are used. (If a team has 2 players, one player has 2 balls of one color and the other player has 2 balls of another color. If a team has 4 players, 2 players have 2 balls each and share one color and the other 2 players have 2 balls each and share another color.)

At the starting sound, one half of the team has to exchange their balls with the other half, so each half of a team ends up with the other half's balls. They have to accomplish this by moving only their chest and body, without touching the boxes with their hands. If a ball falls out of a box, the player can pick it up and put it back in.

This challenge involves a lot of careful stomach maneuvering and is for players 12 or older.

HOW TO MAKE A SWITCHAROO BOX

1. At a pharmacy or supermarket get small corrugated boxes about 6 x 8  by 3–8 inches deep (those are very approximate measurements; anything vaguely close to this would work) that are used for shipping health care products and are thrown out after the shelves are stocked.

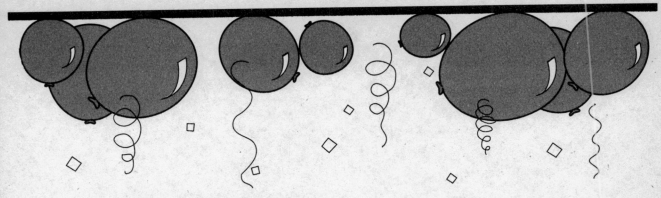

2. If the boxes are flat, open them up and with plastic packaging tape, tape up one end. Cut the flaps off of the other end.

3. Cut off one of the long sides.

4. On the bottom at either end close to the remaining long side make a hole.

5. Thread a 3 foot piece of string or yarn through both holes.

6. With the open sides facing up and out, secure a box under the chin of each player, tying the string snugly around his/her back.

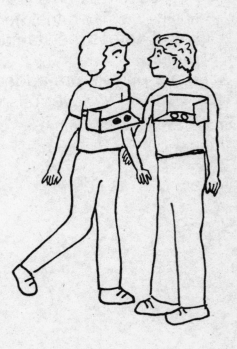

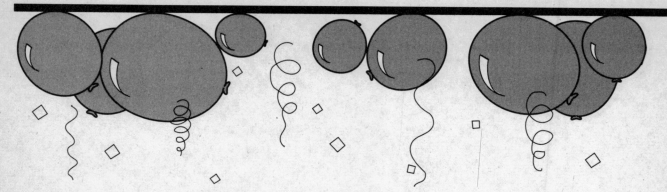

Peanut Relay

Materials for Each Team: 2 peanuts.

Players: Teams of 2 or more players each, or have individuals compete against each other.

How It's Played: With tape or chalk, mark off start and finish lines fifteen feet apart. One player from each team kneels in position behind the starting line with their nose to the floor (make sure it's clean, or put a plastic sheet over it) and a peanut in front of them. The other players kneel on the finish line.

At the starting sound, the players on the starting line use their noses to push the peanut down the track and across the finish line. Then their teammates take over and push it back and across the starting line. The team that does this first wins.

If more players are added to a team, extend the relay and have each new player push the peanut one additional length of the track.

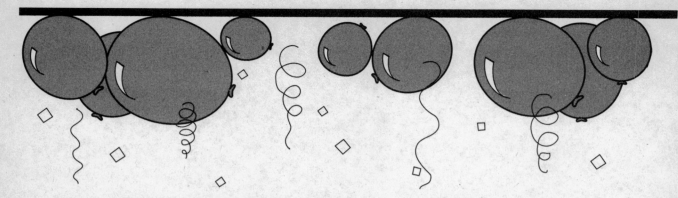

Blow the Pong Down

Materials for Each Player: One ping pong ball with an individual mark or color on it.

Players: Individuals to play against each other.

How It's Played: With tape, mark a track on the floor, weaving around furniture and in and out of rooms. At the beginning of the track mark a starting line and at the end a finish line.

The game starts with each player's ball on the starting line and players on their hands and knees. At the starting sound players have to blow their ball down the track to the finish line. The first player to do this wins. To lengthen the game have the players go back and forth several times.

Make sure the area around the track is wide enough to accommodate all the players. If the track goes around furniture make sure that places where a ball could go under and get lost like coaches, bureaus and desks have strips of poster board covering the bottom.

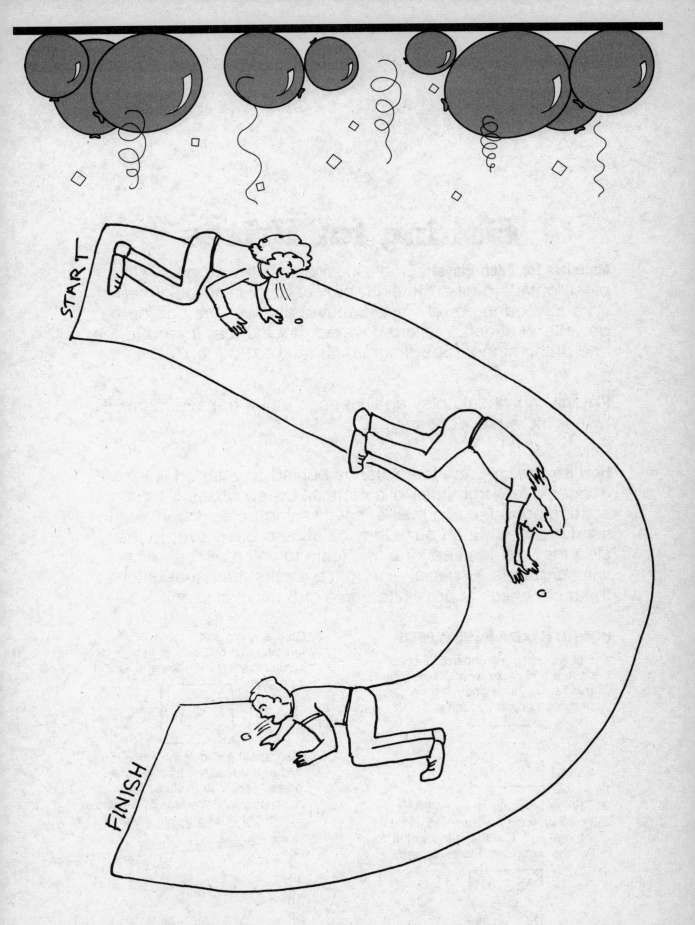

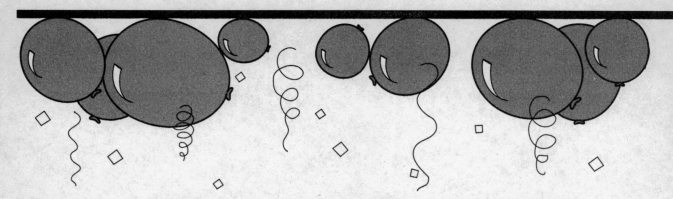

Fishing for Prizes

Materials for Each Player: Small, inexpensive boxed gifts with a piece of Velcro glued to each box, and a fishing pole made from a wooden dowel. Tape 6 feet of string to the end of the dowel and attach a Velcro-covered piece of cardboard to the end of the string. (See diagram on the next page.)

Players: Individuals play against each other, or have teams of two or more players each.

How It's Played: Each team stands behind on a taped line, about six feet from their pile of small boxed prizes. At the starting sound, using their special fishing poles, they have to fish for prizes. Each prize they catch and bring over to their side they get to keep. The first team to catch all their prizes wins and gets a special extra prize (or the team that catches the most prizes in an allotted time of 5 minutes wins).

HOW TO MAKE A FISHING POLE

1. Cut a piece of cardboard 5 inches square and make a small hole in the middle, just large enough for a piece of string to pass through it.

2. Through the hole thread a 5 foot piece of string that has a large knot on one end. Pull the string so the knot is up against the cardboard.

3. Glue 2 velcro strips in an "X" formation on one side of the cardboard. (Use Elmers or a similar type glue).

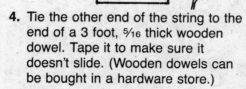

4. Tie the other end of the string to the end of a 3 foot, $5/16$ thick wooden dowel. Tape it to make sure it doesn't slide. (Wooden dowels can be bought in a hardware store.)

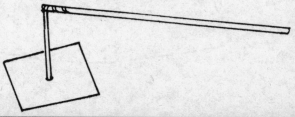

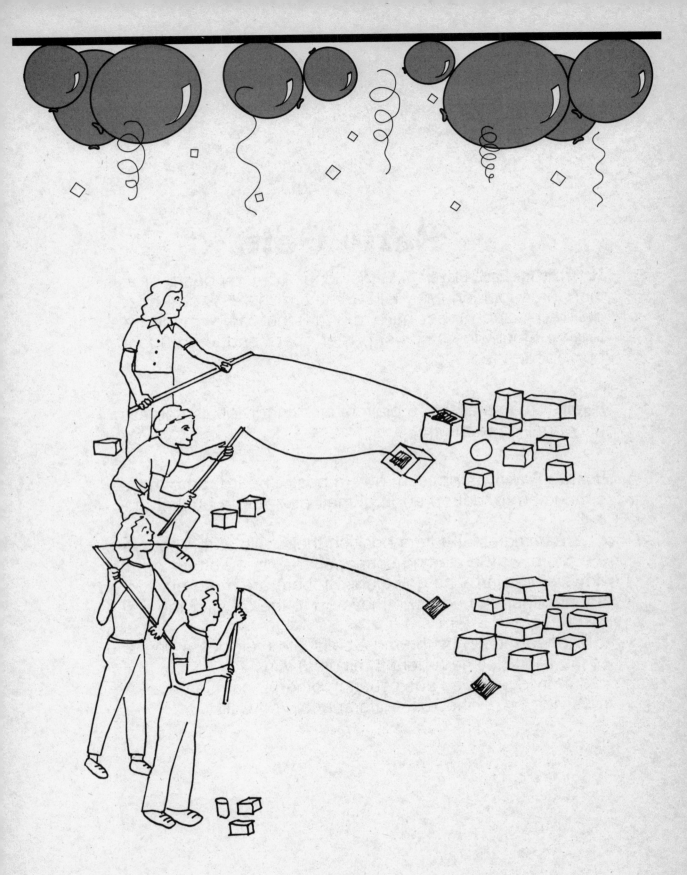

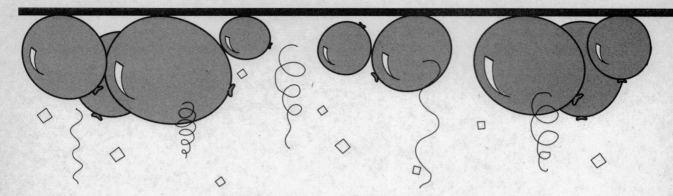

Party Golf

Materials for Each Player: A 3-foot long, 1x2-inch board or a ¾ inch three-foot long dowel. Each team shares 3 or 4 dozen golf ball–sized rubber balls, a 6 to 8 foot ramp (made by taping 2-foot-wide strips of poster board end to end), and a box about a foot high.

Players: Teams of 2 to 6 players each. Individuals can also play against each other.

How It's Played: Each team gets a poster board ramp that's connected to the top edge of their box, and a bucket of balls.

2 teammates at a time position their balls at the bottom of the ramp. At the starting sound, all teams tee off, using their dowels or boards as golf clubs. If there are more players on a team, then the next two move up to tee off after the first two have had a turn.

The team that hits the most balls into their box at the end of the allotted time (about 4 minutes) wins.

If individuals play against each other, 2 can share a receiving box if they use different colored balls.

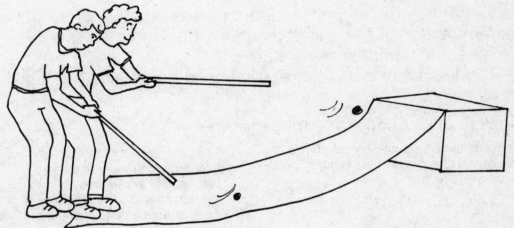

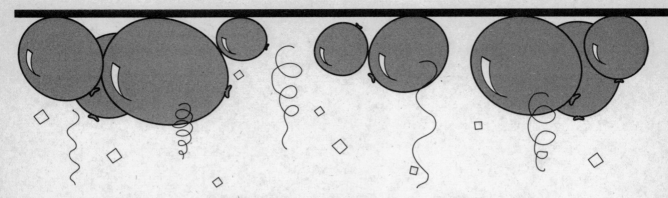

It's a Bird, It's a Plane, It's a Paper Wad

Materials for Each Team: 24 damp paper balls made from single sheets of paper towel (about the size of a golf ball), a bucket hat, and a catapult made from a 6-ounce juice can and a board about 3x18 inches long and one-eighth to one-quarter inch thick. (See diagram below.)

Players: Teams of two players each.

How It's Played: Players kneel on the floor, each with 12 wet paper wads and a catapult, and their teammates stand in front, wearing their bucket hats. At the starting sound, the launcher has to catapult wet paper wads into the air, and the other player has to catch them in the bucket hat. If a wad misses, the launcher may retrieve it.

The team that gets all twelve wads in the bucket hat first wins.

HOW TO MAKE A CATAPULT (with adult supervision)

1. Hammer a long nail through the center of the board just enough to make a hole.

3. Take the nail out of the can and put it through both the board and the can, to hold the two together. With the handle end of the hammer, stick it inside the can and push on the nail bending it away from the opening. Place the paper wad on one end and the player slams down the other end.

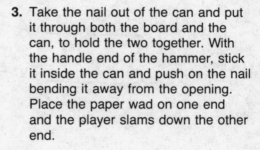

2. Take the nail out of the board and nail it through the side of the can in the center.

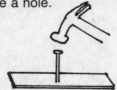

Container Head Relay

Materials for Each Player: Container hats, 6 golf ball-size balls or paper balls.

Players: Teams of 4 or more players each.

How It's Played: The players of each team stand in a row each wearing a container hat. The first player in line on each team has 6 paper balls in their container hat.

At the starting sound they have to transfer those balls to the next player in line's hat without using hands and only moving their head and body. When the balls get to the last player in line they have to be transferred the same way back to the beginning. The first team to do this wins.

To lengthen the game have the teams transfer the balls up and down the line as many times as you think appropriate.

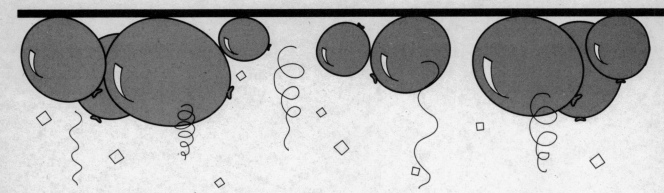

Water Cannon Personal Artillery

Materials for Each Team: A plastic squeezable condiment dispenser, a bucket of water, and a dozen paper cups.

Players: Teams of 2 or more players each.

How It's Played: Each team gets 12 paper cups that will sit as targets on a long table.

The teams stand behind a tape or chalk line about 4 feet from the table. Each player has a squeezable condiment dispenser filled with water, which acts as a high-powered water gun.

At the starting sound, the shooting begins. The first team to knock their paper cups off the table wins. (When their guns run out of water, they can fill them up in their buckets.)

Mark the cups with each team's markings, so there will be no confusion when it's time to score.

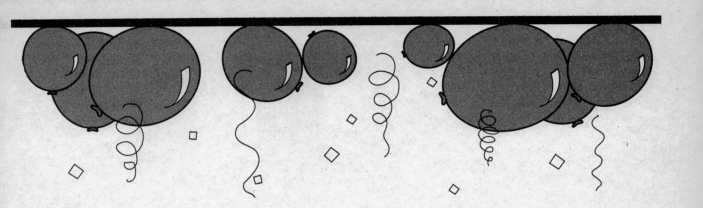

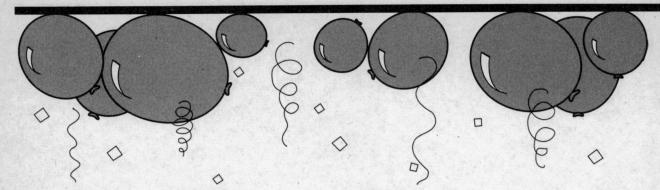

Worm-a-Thon

Materials for Each Team: A big bowl of play dough.

Players: Teams of two or more players. Individuals can also play against each other.

How It's Played: Each team gets a large bowl of play dough. (It's a lot less expensive to make your own than to buy some. See recipe below.) The players sit on the floor. At the starting sound, each team has to make the longest worm possible, by taking pieces of dough, rolling them in between their hands to make long round pieces, then connecting them together.

The team that makes the longest worm in the allotted time (about six or seven minutes) wins.

PLAY DOUGH RECIPE

(Makes 1 big bowl)

In a pot, mix:

3 cups of flour
3 cups of water
1 ½ cups of salt
12 teaspoons of cream of tartar
(add a few drops of food coloring to make it more fun)

Cook over a medium heat until it turns into a doughy consistency, then knead slightly with your hands.

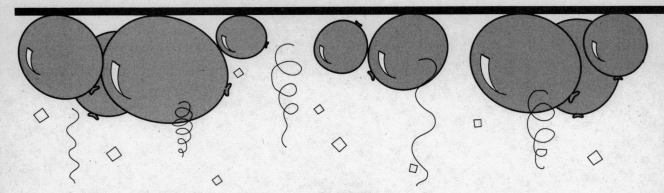

Absorbent Messages

Materials for Each Team: A roll of paper towels, lots of tape (a couple of small rolls or one big one), and a secret message.

Players: Teams of 2 to 3 players each.

How It's Played: To prepare for this challenge, the game master has to come up with different silly messages for each team. For example: "Beware of cats with tiny, little bald faces;" "Eight monkeys from the sacred tombs of Egypt;" "A wagon of wiggly, waggly worms wiggled home." All the messages should have the same number of words.

To prepare each team's message, unravel a roll of paper towels and, with a marker, write the words from the message out of order, one word on a sheet, leaving blank sheets in between. Don't detach any sheets. Now roll up the roll.

The game begins with each team getting a roll of paper towels with a secret message and the same message written on a piece of paper.

At the starting sound, each team has to unravel their roll, find the words to the secret message, tape the sheets together so the message can be read from left to right (without any blank sheets in between), then tape together the blank sheets remaining and roll up the roll. The first team to do this wins.

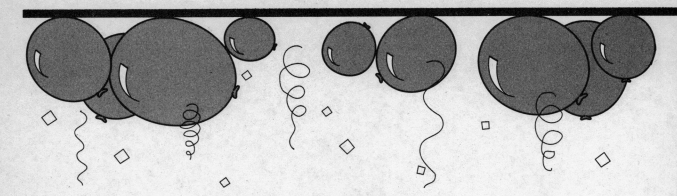

Those Giant Demented Snails

Materials for Each Player: An extra-large plastic trash bag for each player.

Players: Individuals compete against each other, or make teams.

How it's Played: With tape or chalk, mark off start and finish lines fifteen feet apart. The players step into their trash bags, which they hold up to their neck, and lie down on the ground with their heads at the starting line. (Note: Use the strongest bags possible or double up two bags.)

At the starting sound, everyone has to wiggle their way as fast as they can down the track, across the finish line and then back across the starting line. To lengthen the race have players go back and forth several times. The first player or team of players to complete the challenge wins.

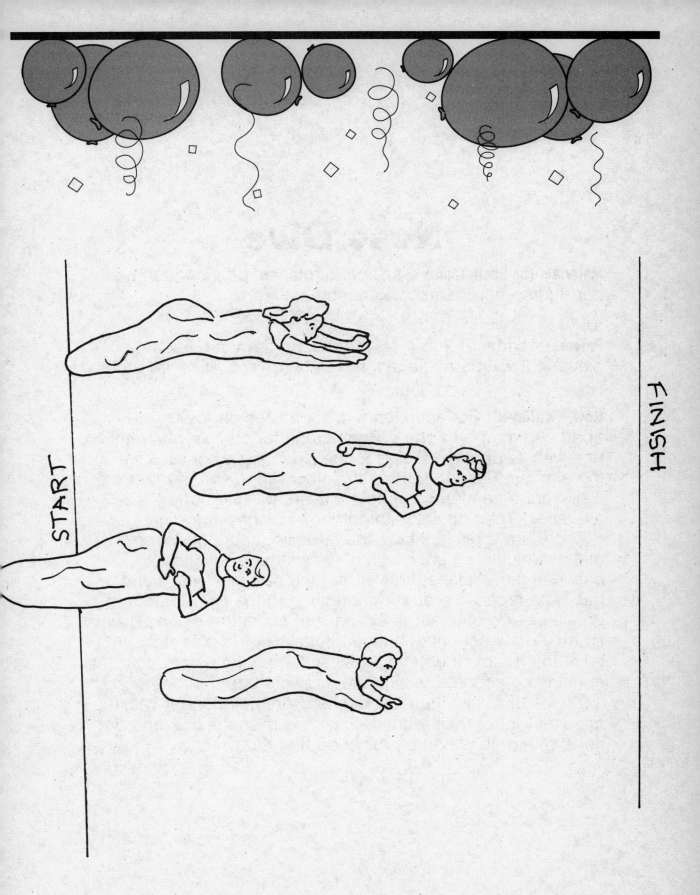

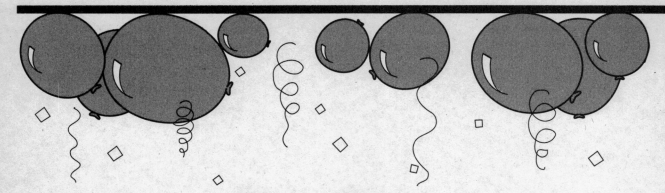

Nose Dive

Materials for Each Team: 24 paper airplanes, a fly swatter, and a corrugated cardboard box, about 2x2 feet.

Players: Teams of 2 to 4 players each. (If a team has 4 players, 2 will be airplane throwers and two will be swatters.)

How It's Played: For each team, mark 2 lines on the floor 6 feet apart using tape or chalk. Behind one taped line, place the box with its opening facing to the side instead of up. This is the airplane hangar. Behind the other taped line (if there are 4 players on a team) stands 2 players with 24 paper airplanes. Their object is to get the airplanes in the hangar.

There are 2 players from the opposing team (it doesn't matter which one) each with a fly swatter, positioned between the airplane thrower and the hangar. They stand behind a taped line at arm's length from the flight path and on either side of it, and their job is to shoot the planes down so they don't get in the hangar. If they swat a plane, they have to crumple it up into a ball so it can't be used again. At the starting sound, the airplane throwers begin throwing and the ones that gets the most airplanes in their hangar within 5 minutes win for their team. If airplanes miss the box and are not swatted, they can be retrieved and thrown again.

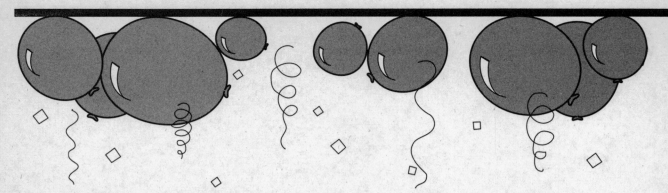

Peanut Butter and Toe Jam

Materials for Each Team: 6 slices of stale bread or toast, a bowl of peanut butter, a bowl of jelly, and one or 2 plastic knives, depending on how many players are on a team.

Players: Teams of 2 or 3 players each.

How It's Played: This game is played on the floor. One player holds a piece of toast down on the floor. The other player has a plastic butter knife, which is held firmly between the toes, dips it into a bowl of peanut butter and spreads it on the toast. Then that player dips the knife into the jam bowl and spreads the jam on the peanut butter. The toast holder tops it off with another piece of toast making a peanut butter and jelly sandwich. (The toast holders also hold the bowls still as their partners dip their knives in it.) The first team to make a three-decker sandwich wins. To lengthen the challenge make the sandwiches higher.

It doesn't matter how much peanut butter and jam is spread on each layer of the sandwich as long as a little gets on.

If a team has 3 players, the third player can be the jam spreader.

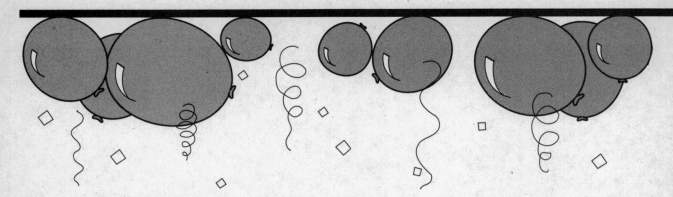

Marshmallow On A Stick

Materials for Each Team: 36 toothpicks, two foot square, two inch thick piece of foam rubber which can be bought in most fabric shops and a large bag of marshmallows.

Players: Teams of 2–5 players each.

How It's Played: Mark off an 8 foot long area with strips of tape at either end. Randomly stick 3 dozen toothpicks in one side of the foam rubber (once they're in, dull the points sticking out so they won't hurt anyone). One player stands behind one taped line and holds the foam rubber in front of their face like a shield with the tooth picks facing out. The other players from that team stand 8 feet away behind the other line with a jumbo size bag of marshmallows. At the starting sound they have to throw their marshmallows at the foam rubber and get them stuck on the toothpicks.

The team with the most impaled marshmallows at the end of the allotted time of 4 minutes wins. Marshmallows that don't hit their mark can be retrieved and thrown again.

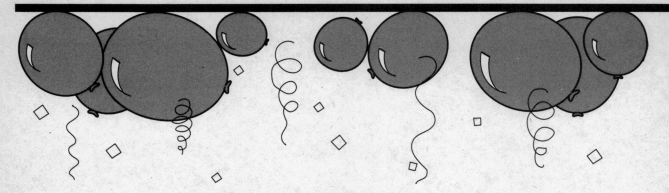

Dizzy Derby

Materials for Each Team: 5 water balloons and a large plastic bucket or plastic-lined box.

Players: Teams of 2 or more players each.

How It's Played: Mark off 2 lines on the floor with tape or chalk 8 feet apart. Behind one line is a bucket that can hold five water balloons and behind the other line are 2 teammates with the water balloons. One player is blindfolded and holds a balloon. At the starting sound, this player is spun around twice and then has to drop the balloon in the bucket 8 feet away. The challenge is for their teammates to give them directions to get to that bucket, because they will be disoriented and slightly dizzy. After one player gets a balloon in the bucket, it's another teammate's turn to be blindfolded, spun around, and carry the balloon, and someone else's turn to give directions.

The first team to get 5 balloons in their bucket wins. To lengthen the game, add more balloons.

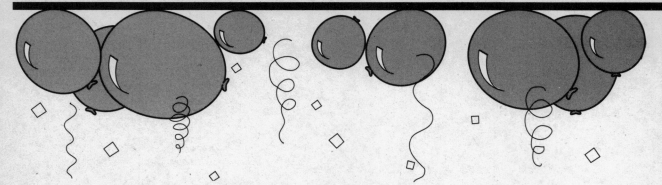

Bowlarama

Materials Needed: A baseball or a rubber ball, 10 empty, jumbo-sized plastic soda bottles.

Players: Teams of 2 to 4 players each. If teams have 4 or 5 players, keep the number of teams down to 3 or 4.

How It's Played: This is a simplified bowling game using plastic soda bottles as pins and a baseball or a rubber ball for the bowling ball. You will need 2 assistants to quickly set up pins every time they are knocked down. To maintain the triangular shape of the pin formation and expedite setting up the pins, a triangular piece of poster board with circles indicating where the pins should stand could be placed on the floor.

The bowler should stand behind a taped line, about fifteen feet from the pins. Each player from a team gets one chance to roll. One point is given for each pin knocked over. When every player from a team has had a chance to roll, then the ball goes to the next team. You decide how many rounds the game should go depending on how many teams are playing and how many players are on each team.

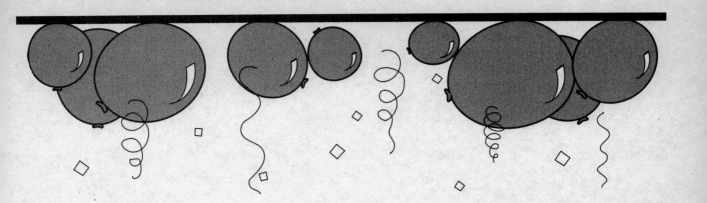

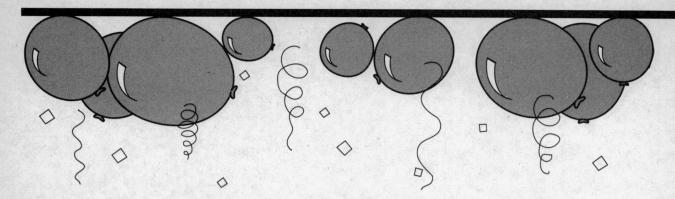

Rebound Ball

Materials for Each Team: One dozen rubber balls about the size of golf balls, and a bucket hat.

Players: Teams of 3 players each.

How It's Played: Each team gets 12 small rubber balls. Mark 2 lines on the floor, about 10 feet apart. One player from each team wears a bucket hat and stands behind one line. The other players from that team stand behind the other line. They have to bounce their balls, one at a time, off the ground, and try to get it into the bucket hat. The bucket-hat wearer will have to bend down and move from side to side to help get balls into the bucket. If a ball misses, it can be retrieved and thrown again.

The first team to get all 12 balls in their team's bucket hat wins.

Note: Change the number of balls if you want the game to be longer or shorter.

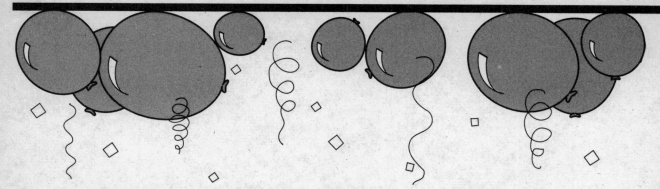

Spider Web Prize Hunt

Materials Needed: Lots of string and a prize for each player.

Players: For individuals

How It's Played: Make string trails, one for each guest, that meander and intertwine, throughout the house—maybe even outside, too. At the central starting point, attach rolled-up paper plates to the ends of each string (for rolling up the string trails), and write the name of a guest on each one. At the end of each string trail is a small prize.

At the starting sound, players begin rolling up their webs. The first player to find the prize wins and gets an extra gift.

Note: Since string will be everywhere, it's a good idea to play this game as soon as your guests arrive.

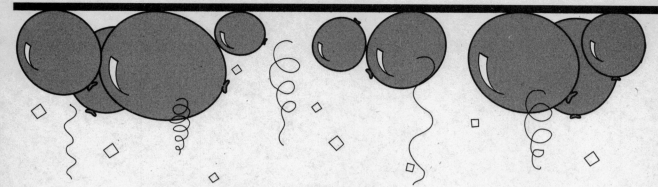

Sneaky Feet

Materials for Each Player: 2 small corrugated cardboard boxes, roughly 5x8 inches (these are the sneaky feet—see description below), and 20 paper balls, use different colors for each player or team. (If teams are playing, allow fewer balls for each player.)

Players: Individuals compete against each other, or have teams of 2 to 4 players each.

How It's Played: Using strips of white tape as markers set up start and finish lines on the floor, 10 to 15 feet apart. Each player wears a pair of sneaky feet. On the floor within the taped area, spread around the colored paper balls. At the starting sound, each team enters the track area from behind the starting line, collects their team's balls underneath their sneaky feet and drags them past the finish line. The first team to do this wins.

HOW TO MAKE SNEAKY FEET

1. At a pharmacy or food market get small corrugated cardboard boxes about 16x8x3–8 inches deep. If the boxes have been broken down and are flat, open them up and use plastic packaging tape to tape up one end. (These are approximate measurements; anything vaguely close to this would work and the boxes don't all have to be the same size.)

2. Push the flaps on the other end of the box in. If the flaps have already been cut off, that's O.K.

3. From a scrap of corrugated cardboard, cut a piece that's slightly bigger than the top of the box and tape it to the top, closed side. This is for extra strength.

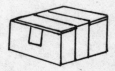

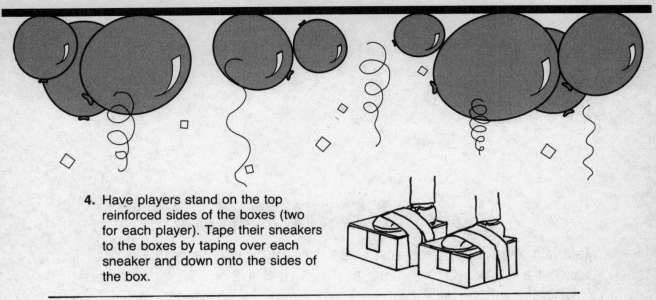

4. Have players stand on the top reinforced sides of the boxes (two for each player). Tape their sneakers to the boxes by taping over each sneaker and down onto the sides of the box.

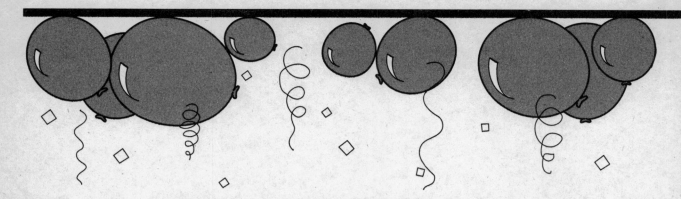

Speed Ball Relay

Materials Needed for Each Team: 24 rubber or paper balls in a box on a chair. (Crunch up a sheet of 8 1/2 x 11 paper into a tight ball).

Players: For large teams of 6 or more. The bigger, the more fun.

How the Game is Played: Each team lines up facing forward, player to player with their hands almost touching. On one chair is a box of balls. At the starting sound the team player first in line on the left picks up a ball with the left hand, then passes it to the right hand, then hands it to the second player-in-line's left hand, who transfers it to the right hand, and the process continues as fast as possible until all 12 balls have gone all the way down the line to the last player's right hand and back down the line again and into the box they originated from.

This is where the fun comes in: while balls are still making the first pass down the line in one direction, balls will be returning going in the opposite direction. Good luck!

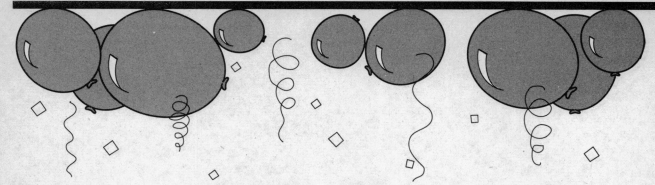

Stuff-a-Thon

Materials Needed: Large bags of marshmallows and plastic quart-sized deli or freezer containers.

Players: Individuals compete against each other.

How It's Played: This game is extremely simple and lots of fun. Each player gets a quart-sized plastic container with a lid and a large bag of marshmallows, which they can share with a player next to them.

At the starting sound, players try to stuff as many marshmallows in to the container as possible and still be able to put the lid on. The player with the most marshmallows stuffed at the end of 2 minutes wins. (Winning at this game is going to take a lot of marshmallow squashing.)

Make sure you give each player more than enough marshmallows to fill a container.

For an extra treat, everyone can take what they stuffed home with them.

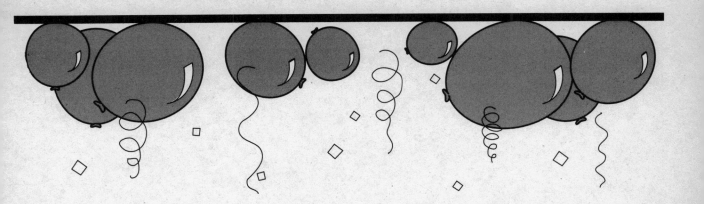

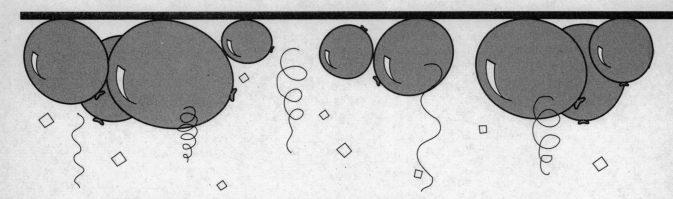

Marshmallow Missiles

Materials for Each Team: A bucket hat, a large bag of marshmallows, and a fly swatter.

Players: Teams of 2 to 5 players each.

How It's Played: One team player wears a bucket hat. The other team player stands about 6 feet away behind a tape or chalk line and, using a fly swatter, tries to swat marshmallows into the bucket. The player wearing the bucket hat can move around but can't cross the line. The team that gets the most marshmallows into their bucket within 4 minutes wins. (The player with the bucket hat should wear goggles.)

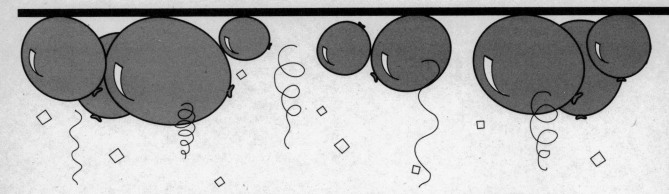

Paper Cup Pyramid

Materials for Each Team: Four dozen paper cups. (You can buy a large quantity inexpensively at a restaurant supplier.)

Players: Individual players compete against each other, or have teams of 2 to 4 players each.

How It's Played: Each team gets four dozen cups and uses them to build a pyramid by placing one layer of cups on top of the other—like a pyramid.

The team that builds the tallest pyramid in the allotted time of five minutes wins. This will take some strategy. To make it even more challenging, have one player from each team sit in a chair wearing a flat-top hat and have the rest of the team build the mountain on their teammate's head.

Flipper It

Materials for Each Team: A bucket of 36 paper balls (paper crumpled into small tight wads the size of golf balls) and 2 sets of swimming flippers for each three-man team (or make flipper feet by taping corrugated cardboard to the bottoms of a player's shoes.

Players: Teams of 3 players each.

How It's Played: With tape or chalk, mark off start and finish lines on the floor 8 feet apart. 2 players wearing flipper feet lie on their backs in a line, one behind the other, with their feet in the air and their heads pointing towards the starting line. The back of one player's head is on the starting line, while the other player's head is 2 feet away from the first player's feet.

The third teammate stands on the starting line with a bucket of paper balls and at the signal, starts throwing the balls at the player's feet whose head is on the starting line. This player hits the balls with their feet to the second player lying down, who then hits the balls over the finish line with their feet. The team that gets the most balls over the finish line in four minutes wins. Balls that miss can be retrieved and thrown again.

Each team should have differently colored paper balls, to make keeping score easier.

HOW TO MAKE FLIPPER FEET

1. Cut two pieces of cardboard, each 8½ x 11 inches, and places them so the short sides are at top and bottom.

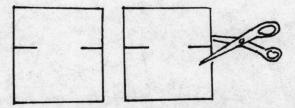

2. On each long side cut a two inch line perpendicular to the side, five inches from the top.

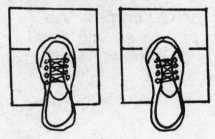

3. Place each of the players' sneakers on a separate sheet, so the toes are in between the cut lines.

4. Now fold the flaps up and tape them to the sides of the sneakers, by wrapping tape completely around the sneakers.

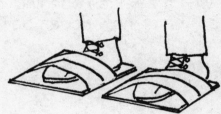

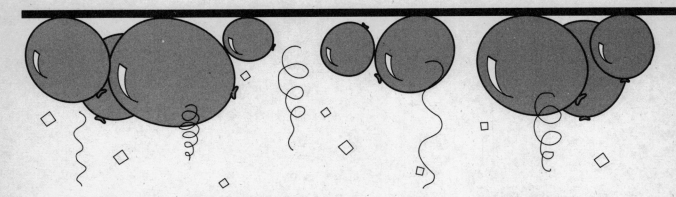

Toilet Tissue Tunnel

Materials for Each Team: A 3-foot long tube (an old carpet tube, or pieces of poster board taped together and rolled into a tube with a 2½-inch opening will work), a roll of toilet tissue, and a 3-foot long wooden dowel.

Players: Teams of 2 players each.

How It's Played: The 2 teammates are stationed one at either end of a tube. At the starting sound, the player that has the roll of toilet paper has to unravel the roll and stuff it in and through the tube with the dowel. The player on the other side has to help pull it out. The first team that passes their entire roll through the tube wins. If the toilet paper breaks during the process, just keep going.

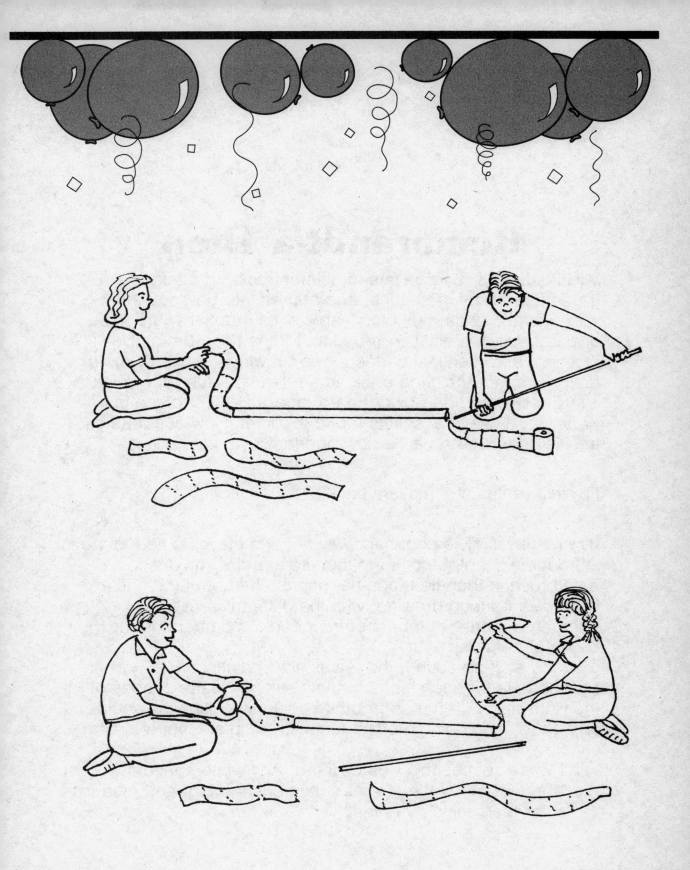

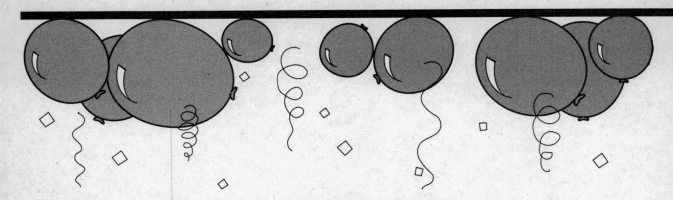

Rembrandt-a-Thon

Materials Needed: 6 large jars of different-colored poster paint (to be shared by the teams) and poured into bowls, 2-inch wide paintbrushes (buy disposable ones in a hardware store or paint shop), a plastic drop cloth for the floor, protective clothing, and identical cartoon-style drawings. (Use a simple drawing from a coloring book as a reference and reproduce it larger by hand on poster board, or a 3 x 3-foot piece of paper, or on several sheets taped together. How accurate or artistic your drawing is, is not important.)

Players: Teams of 2 players each.

How It's Played: The right-hand wrist of one player is tied to the left-hand wrist of the other teammate and they hold a paintbrush in their tied-together hands. In front of them is an oversized cartoon drawing, with the different sections numbered. These numbers correspond to numbers on the bowls of paint.

At the starting sound, the teams start painting. The challenge is for each team to completely fill in the spaces of their drawing with the appropriate colors just like you would in paint-by-numbers. The first team to complete their painting wins.

All white spaces must be covered. Any white space that can't be hidden by the referee's thumb is too big, and means the other team wins by default.

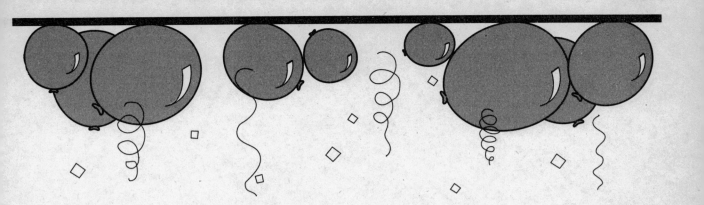

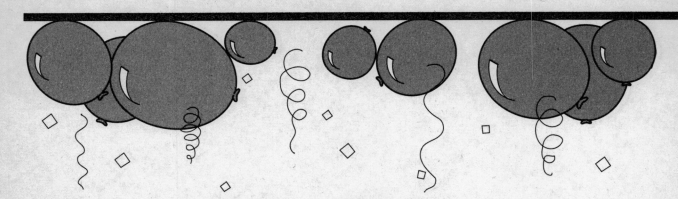

Super Straw

Materials for Each Player: 5 straws, a bowl filled with a quart of fruit juice, soda, or water, and an empty bowl.

Players: Individual players compete against each other, or teams.

How It's Played: Each player has 3 to 5 straws taped together. At the starting sound, they have to suck up the water or soda from one bowl and transfer it to the empty bowl 3 feet away. (Test beforehand to see if the players have enough strength to use five straws to suck up the liquid. But remember, they only need to transport a little at a time. So if five is too many, make it four or three, but don't make it too easy.) The first player or team of players to transfer all their liquid wins. (Make sure all players start off with an equal amount.)

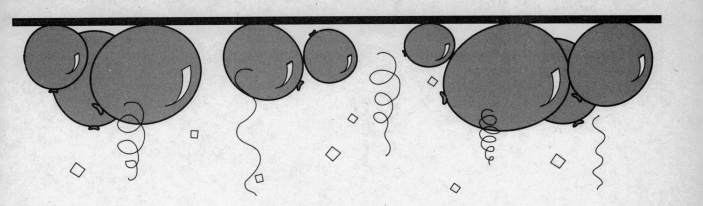

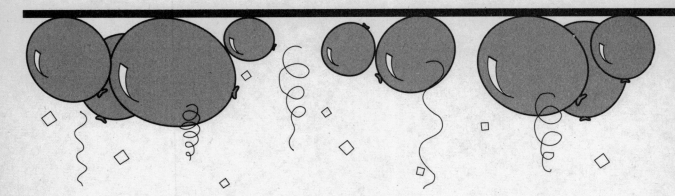

With a Cherry on Top

Materials for Each Team: One whipped cream pie (a disposable aluminum pie plate filled with whipped cream will do), 5 long-stemmed cherries, a plastic covering for the floor, and blankets or gym mats underneath the plastic.

Players: Teams of 2 or more players each. (This game might be best suited for more athletic children.)

How It's Played: One player holds a teammate's ankles wheelbarrow style, and they are positioned behind a taped line on the floor. In front of each team, 5 feet away, is a row of five long-stemmed cherries. 5 feet away from that is a whipped cream pie (one for each team). At the starting sound, the human wheelbarrow has to go to the cherries, pick one up with his/her teeth, and deposit it on the pie. Then they go back and one by one pick up the others, repeating this process until they have put all 5 cherries on the pie. The team that does this first wins.

If more players are added to a team, there must be an even number because it takes at least 2 kids to make a wheelbarrow. Increase the number of cherries for each additional human wheelbarrow, but use the same pie. Make sure there is plenty of space to move around.

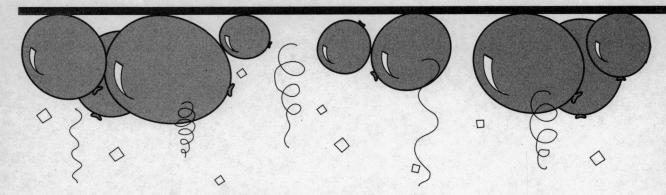

Balloonatic

Materials for Each Team: A large box about 2 feet deep, a roll of tape, and a dozen different-sized balloons.

Players: Individuals play against each other, or have teams of 2 players each.

How It's Played: Each team gets an open box of the same size and the same assortment of different-sized balloons—from about 4 inches to 12 inches wide. The object of the game is for each team or player to get the most balloons possible in their box and get the top taped shut within the allotted time of three minutes. To make it even more fun, place the balloons in an area 10 feet away from the boxes, and have the players run to that area, bringing back one balloon at a time.

Make sure each team starts out with more balloons than needed to fill their box. This will give them the opportunity to pick and choose.

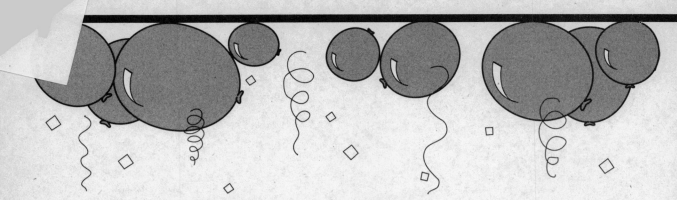

Back-o-Matic

Materials for Each Team: 2 plastic–lined cardboard boxes, eight large water balloons, and a plastic sheet to cover the floor—in case a balloon breaks.

Players: Teams of 2, 4, or 6 players each. It must be an even number.

How It's Played: With tape or chalk, mark off start and finish lines on the floor, ten to fifteen feet apart. Each team is positioned behind the starting line. At the starting sound, 2 teammates take a balloon out of the bag and position it between their backs, so they are standing back to back with the balloon suspended between them.

The challenge is to cross the finish line as fast as possible and drop the balloon in the receiving box. Then they run back, cross the starting line, get another balloon, and continue the process. The first team to transport five balloons from one end of the track to the other wins. The 3 extra balloons are for possible breaks.

If there are more than 2 players on a team, then the other pairs of players take turns transporting a balloon, like a relay race.

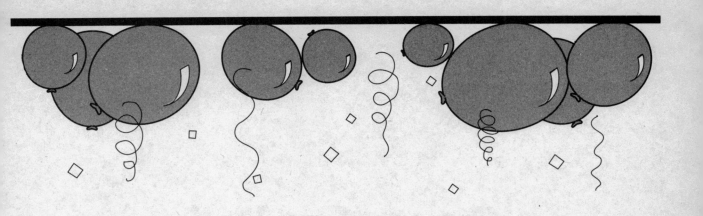

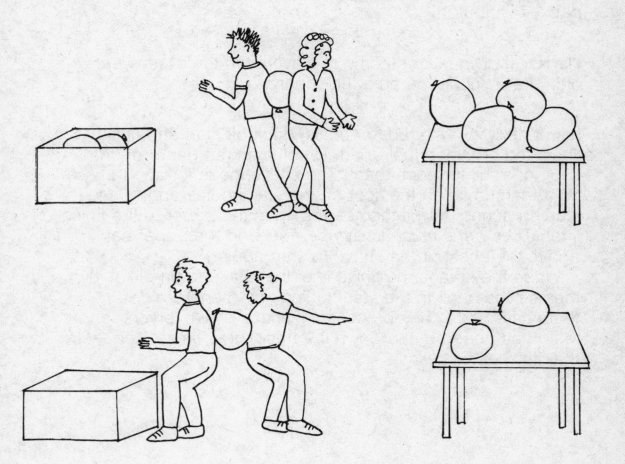

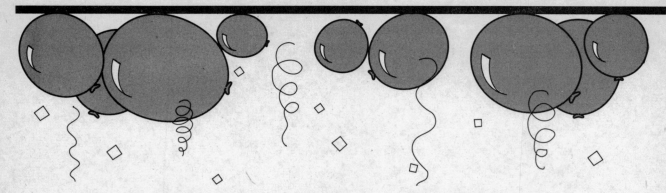

Human Egg Roll

Materials for Each Team: A 10- or 15-foot long piece of kraft paper 3 feet wide. (You can buy a roll of kraft paper at a paper distributor.)

Players: Individuals or teams of players ten to sixteen years old. There should be an adult supervising.

How It's Played: With tape or chalk, mark off start and finish lines, ten or fifteen feet apart. Unroll the kraft paper on the floor, one roll for each team. The challenge is for each player on a team to lie on the floor on the starting line and, at the starting sound, to roll themselves up in the paper to the finish line. (*Their arms must always be free*, and the paper can't go above the chest or they have to start again.)

When they reach the finish line, they have to unroll themselves back to the starting line and then it's a teammate's turn. This process continues until everyone on a team has gone up and down the track three times. The team that finishes first wins.

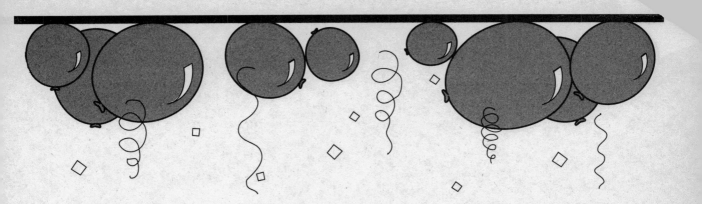

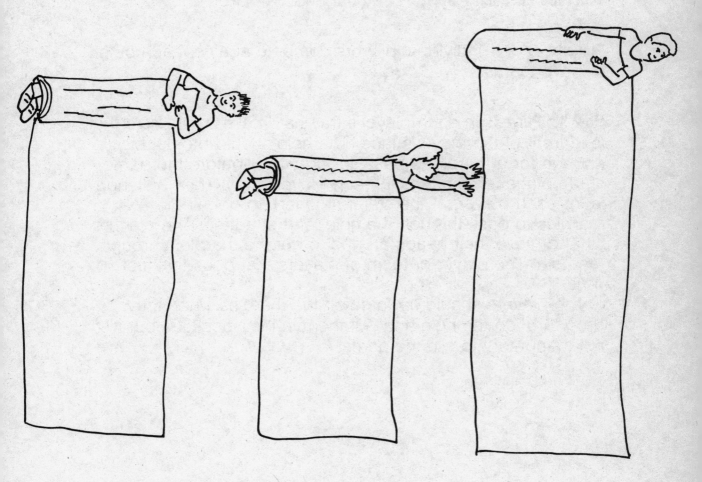

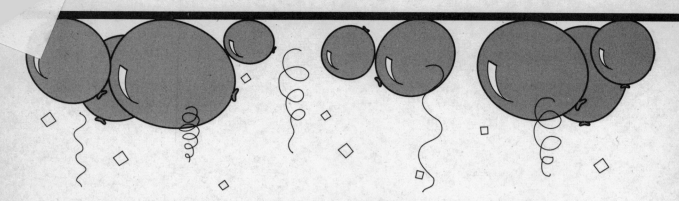

Lose Your Marbles

Materials for Each Player: A tray hat and 10 marbles.

Players: 3 or 4 individual players compete against each other, or have teams.

How It's Played: In each player's tray hat, make a little hole that is in front of the player's face. The hole should be just big enough for a marble to pass through. Just before the game starts place ten marbles in each player's tray. The challenge is for each player, at the starting sound, to get all the marbles to pass through the hole, one at a time. The players tilt and move their heads around to get the marbles through the hole. The player or team of players that does this first wins.

The players should try to catch the marbles when they drop through the hole and put them in their pockets, but it's not mandatory to win the game.

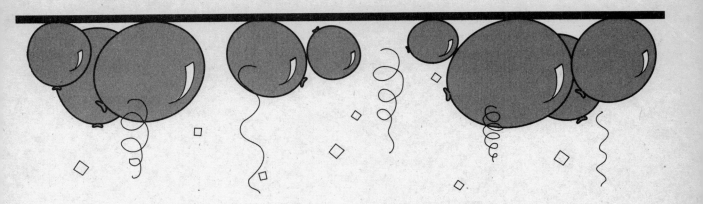

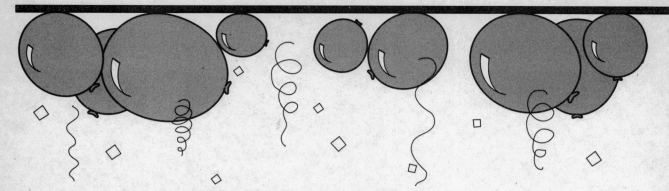

Talented Toes

Materials for Each Player: A box or bucket and 25 paper balls made from tightly crumpled up sheets of eight-and-one-half by eleven-inch paper.

Players: Individual players, or have teams of 2 or more players each.

How It's Played: Tape off a square area on the floor within for each team and place about six feet squared it the paper balls. Have each player remove the shoe and sock from one foot. Their challenge is to pick up the paper balls using only their toes and, by hopping on one leg, bring them to their team's box, which is 6 feet away from the marked—off area.

   The first team to deposit all their balls in their box wins. You can also structure the game so the team that deposits the most balls in 5 minutes wins. The more players involved, the more paper balls you'll need.

   An alternative way of setting up this game is by taping off one large area on the floor that all the teams will use. Assign each team different colored paper balls so you can easily keep track of what each team scored.

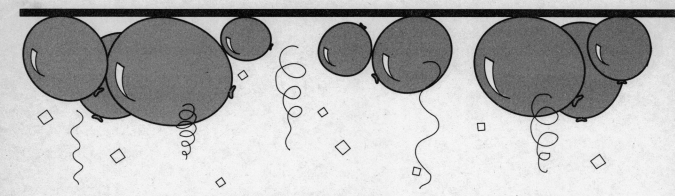

Paper Wad Sharpshooters

Materials for Each Team: A table, a bowl of water, a roll of toilet paper or a box of Kleenex, and a large piece of poster board or paper about three by 3 feet wide (tape several sheets together if needed).

Players: Individual players compete against each or have teams of no more than 4 players each.

How It's Played: With a wide-tipped marker, draw a target on a piece of poster board that consists of 3 concentric circles representing different scores. Tape or tack it to the wall. Mark a line 10 feet away, behind which the players or teams will kneel with their bowls of water and Kleenex.

At the starting sound, the teams have to wet the Kleenex, make balls the size of ping-pong balls or smaller, and throw these at the target. The ones that stick count as a score. The team that scores the most points in 3 minutes win.

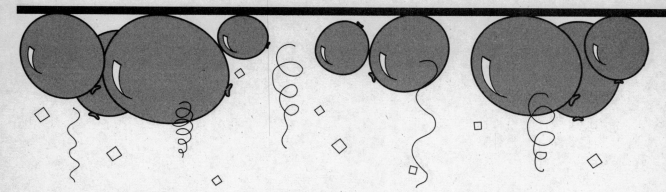

Time to Make the Pies

Materials for Each Team: A table, 10 or more disposable pie plates, a large can of chocolate sauce, a can of whipped cream, a bowl of chopped nuts, and a handful of cherries. (If the game is played on the floor, you'll need a plastic drop cloth.)

Players: Teams of 4 or more players each.

How It's Played: Players from the same team sit or kneel side by side on the floor. The first team member has a stack of pie plates and the whipped cream, the second one has the chocolate sauce, the third one has the nuts, and the fourth has the cherries. If players are added to a team, each one gets a different, new ingredient.

At the starting sound, the first team member fills a pie plate with whipped cream and passes it down the line for each player to add their ingredient. The team that completes the most pies in 3 minutes wins. The game master will check to make sure the winning team's pies include all the ingredients even if it's just a little bit of each, except for the whipped cream, which should fill the pie tin up to its edge.

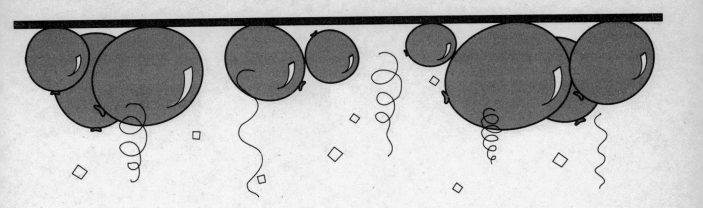

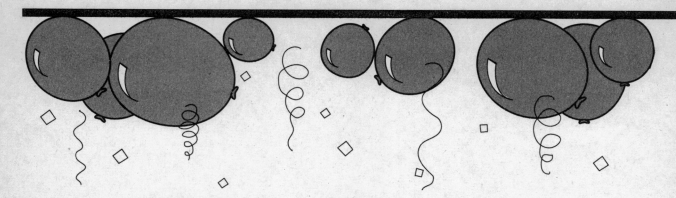

Marathon Dressing

Materials for Each Player: 5 to 10 T-shirts.

Players: Individuals compete against each other, or have teams of 2 or more players each.

How It's Played: In front of each player or team is piled the same number of T-shirts. At the starting sound, each team has to put on all the T-shirts in front of them, one over the other. The first team to do this wins.

The more T-shirts used in this game the more fun it will be. Another way to play is to have the players from each team line up in a row with the pile of T-shirts at one end. At the starting sound, the first player in line has to put all the T-shirts on as fast as possible, then take them off and pass them on to the next player in line, who does the same, until everyone on the team has put on and taken off all the T-shirts. The first team to do this wins. (Hint: As soon as a T-shirt is taken off, the next player should put it on.)

Note: To keep your expenses down, you may be able to buy a pile of secondhand T-shirts at a Goodwill or Salvation Army Thrift Shop.

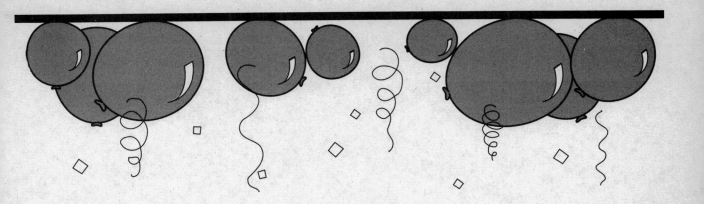

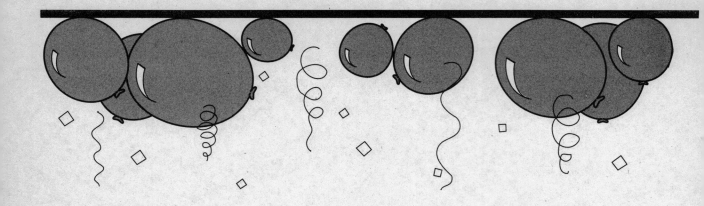

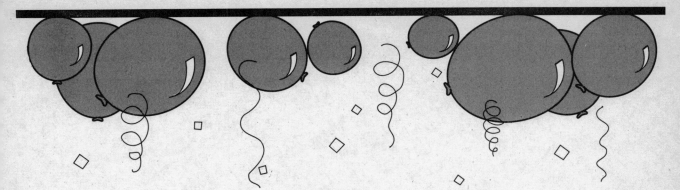

Outdoor Games

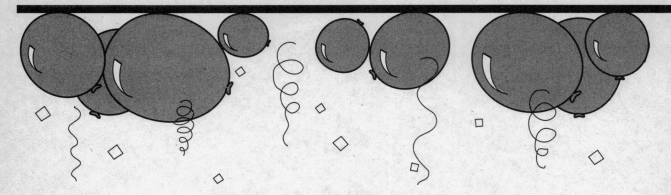

Egg-It-On

Materials for Each Player on a Team: 3 eggs.

Players: An even number of teams of 3 or more players each.

How It's Played: With chalk, set up 2 lines on a field, about 15 to 25 feet apart. Each player on a team starts out with 3 eggs. Each team stands behind their eggs, which rest on their line, on opposite sides of the field. At the starting sound, each team has to gently kick their eggs across the field and over the line on the other side. The first team to do this wins that round. If an egg breaks (cracks are O.K.), that player has to go back to the starting line and get another egg. The team that wins 3 out of 5 rounds wins the game.

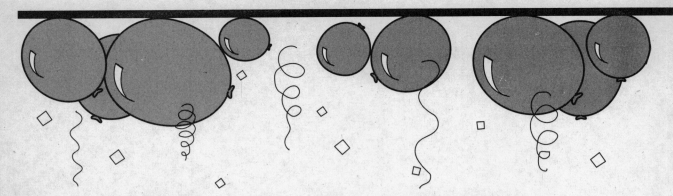

Slippery Soap Relay

Materials For Each Team: A bar of soap for each player, and a plastic drop cloth.

Players: Teams of 3 or more players each. This can also be played by individuals playing against each other; 4 or more make it extra fun.

How It's Played: This game should be played on a plastic sheet on top of a grassy area which will act as a cushion if anyone falls.

With tape, mark off a start and a finish line 15-feet apart. Half of a team stands behind one line and the other half stands behind the other line. If there is an odd number of players on a team, the extra player stands behind the starting line. The referee should give each player on a team a number so they know their order in the relay.

Each team gets a wet bar of soap which rests on the starting line. At the starting sound, a player has to propel their soap bar down the track by adding pressure with one bare foot on the top end of the soap. Kicking is not allowed. When the soap crosses the finish line a teammate from that side has to propel the soap back to the starting line and the third teammate takes over and the process continues.

The first team that gets the soap down and back 10 times wins. This is a slippery game so be careful.

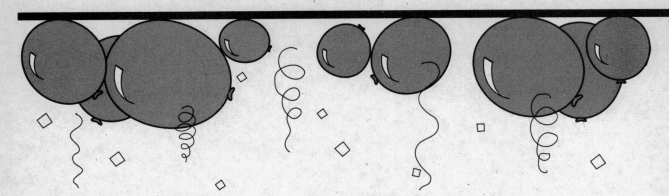

Dinosaur Bones

Materials for Each Team: A dozen dog bone biscuits (dinosaur bones) and a kiddy pool filled with mud.

Players: Teams of 2 or 3 players each. If there are more than 3 players each it will get too crowded.

How It's Played: In a kiddy pool filled with 3 or 4 inches of mud (or in a sand box) hide one or two dozen dog bone biscuits. At the starting sound, each team has to wade through the mud or sand searching for ancient fossils. (Mud is more fun.)

The team that finds the most bones in the allotted time of three minutes wins. To lengthen the challenge, play for 3 out of 5 rounds.

The number of bones you hide in the mud depends on how many are playing. Make sure you bury them right before the game begins so they don't get too soft.

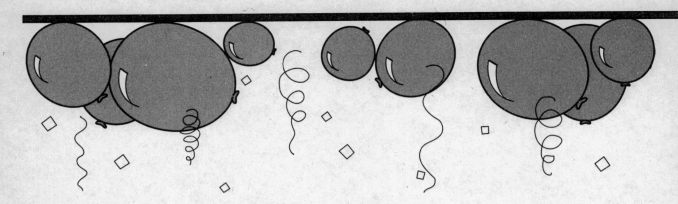

Sinking Ships

Materials Needed: A tub of water or a kiddy wading pool, a squirt gun, and a tissue box ship, for each player.

Players: 2 teams of 2 or 3 players each, or have individuals play against each other.

How It's Played: Each player on a team gets a squirt gun and a ship. Each ship should be marked with its owner's initials. The challenge is to sink your ship using the squirt gun. The team that sinks all of their ships first wins. Once players sink their own ships, they can help sink a teammate's ship. When a gun runs out of water, it can be refilled in the pool.

HOW TO MAKE A CARDBOARD SAILBOAT

1. Get an empty tissue box.

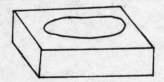

2. Cut a piece of cardboard in a triangle shape for the sail. The bottom of the sail should be as long as the opening on the box.

3. Cut a short slot at one end of the box to accommodate the sail.

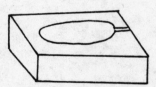

4. Place the sail in the box and push it down to the bottom and into the slot. Now secure it with tape.

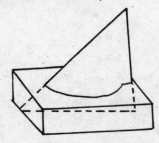

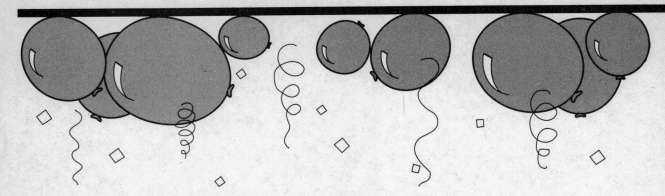

Tying One On

Materials for Each Team: All team players must wear laced sneakers.

Players: Teams of 3 players each.

How It's Played: With tape or chalk, mark off three, 4 x 4 foot bases, approximately ten to fifteen feet apart in a triangle formation. Have each player untie their shoelaces, and then position one player from each team on each base.

At the starting sound, the players on base number one run to base number two and tie their right sneaker to their teammate's left sneaker. Then they have to hobble as fast as they can to base number 3, where ties their player number 2 right-foot shoelace to the left-foot shoelace of the third base player. Now all 3 players are tied together, and they have to hobble as fast as they can back to home base. The first team to do this wins. To lengthen the challenge play for the best out of 5 rounds.

Make sure each base is large enough to accommodate the players from all the teams or make several sets of bases.

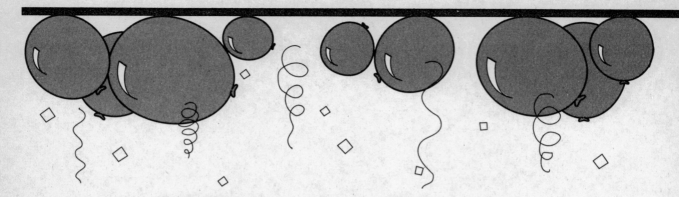

Silly String Sprint

Materials for Each Player: A can of Silly String.

Players: Individual players to compete against each other.

How It's Played: With chalk or tape, outline a circular track or one that weaves around. Mark off a start and a finish line. The players kneel on the starting line holding a Silly String can with the nozzle touching the ground.

At the starting sound, the players race around the track making a Silly String trail. It's important that there is enough room so nobody crosses over and breaks somebody else's trail. (If not, have one set of players go first and the others go later.) The first player to make it twice around the track and cross the finish line, without a break in their Silly String, wins. If the string breaks, the player can patch it.

This game can be played indoors if there is enough space so the players don't get in each other's way.

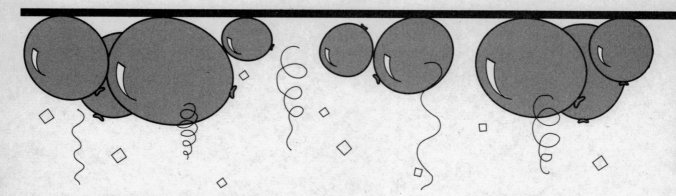

Old-Fashioned Egg Race

Materials for Each Player: 6 eggs and a spoon, and at least a 15-foot long running track—indoors or out.

Players: This game is for single players to play against each other. It's more fun when you have at least 3 or more competing.

How It's Played: This game is zillions of years old and is just as much fun as the newer ones.

Each player holds a spoon and has one toe of one foot touching the starting line. At the sound of "go," the players have to run to another line, 15 to 30 feet away, where the eggs are, pick up an egg with their spoons and bring it back to the starting point. The first player to transport all 6 eggs unbroken wins.

To shorten or lengthen the game, you can vary the number of eggs that have to be picked up. You can also alter the game by having the player start out with their eggs and bring them to a finish line, or have a team competition by making it a relay race.

This can be played indoors by shortening the track and laying plastic sheets on the floor in case of broken eggs.

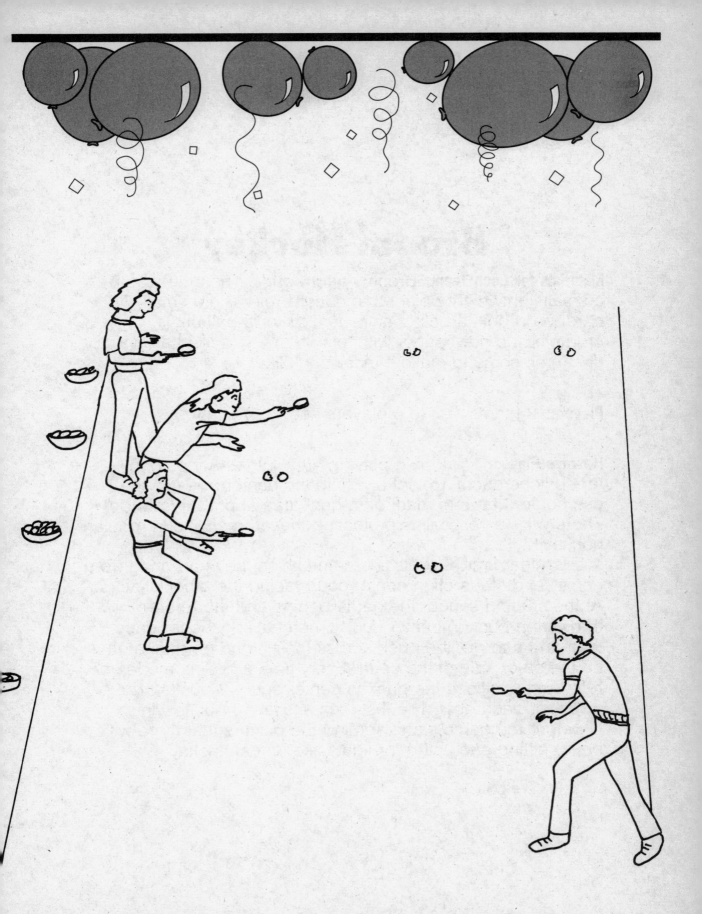

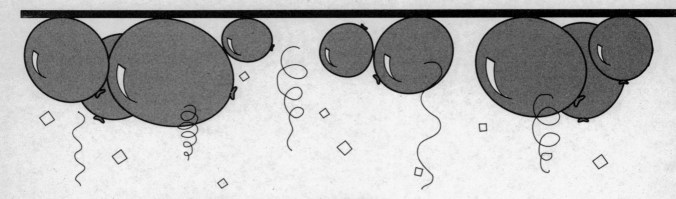

Broom Hockey

Materials for Each Team: Brooms and a puck. The puck can be a small lightweight object that doesn't roll—like a small cardboard box, a ball of aluminum foil or a ball of crumpled-up newspaper with lots of tape wrapped around it. (Flatten it some to make it more puck like)

Players: 2 teams of 3 to 5 players each.

How It's Played: Mark off a playing area with 2, 8-foot long taped lines about 15 feet apart. In the center of each line, use colored tape to mark off a goal area about 3 feet wide. There will be no goalies protecting these areas like in regular hockey.

Each team player gets a broom (which they can bring from home) and starts off in center court facing the other players. At the starting sound, the game begins and the referee throws the puck in center court. The challenge is for each team to try to get the puck across their taped-off goal area on the other side of the court. Every time a goal is made, the referee repositions the puck in center court. 2 points are given for each goal. The first team to get 10 points wins.

Before the game starts, remind the players that there will be no hitting each other or fights like in real hockey.

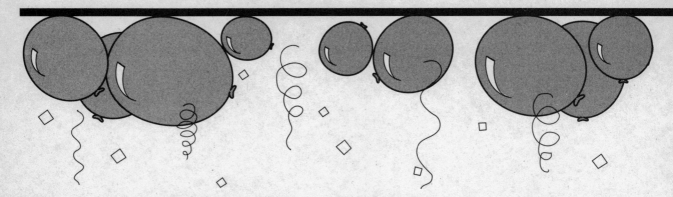

Up, Up, and Away

Materials Needed: A small tank of helium capable of inflating at least fifty balloons, two dozen 2-foot long pieces of string, something lightweight like a couple of rolled-up sheets of newspaper, balloons, and large plastic trash bags.

Players: Teams of 3 players each.

How It's Played: Have helium-filled balloons in large plastic trash bags that are anchored to the ground. At the starting sound, each team has to get their roll of newspaper off the ground by tying helium balloons to it. The first team to do this wins. One player from a team retrieves a balloon from the bag, another ties a piece of string to it, and the third ties it to their object. (Before the game, test to see if the object you have chosen can be lifted by 12 or fewer balloons.)
   Make sure all the teams have objects of equal weight.

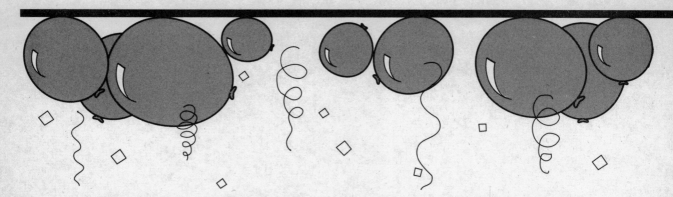

Water Balloon Volleyball

Materials Needed: A volleyball net and 11 water balloons.

Players: 2 teams with at least 2 players on each team. (The more players on a team, the better). For ages 10 and older.

How It's Played: A coin is flipped to see who goes first, then the referee hands the captain of the starting team a water balloon. The captain throws it over the net, and the other team hits it back, like in volleyball. The volley continues until the balloon breaks, which is a point for the opposite team. The next balloon starts out with the scoring team. If a balloon lands on the ground, it can be picked up. After 11 balloons have been broken or when the allotted time of 10 to 20 minutes is up, tally the score. (This is a good game to play in bathing suits.)

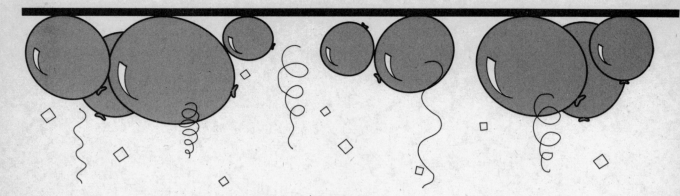

Airborne

Materials for Each Team: A beach ball.

Players: 2 or more teams of 4 or more players each.

How It's Played: Each team stands in a circle about 8 feet in diameter. (If you use a smaller ball, move the players closer together.) At the starting sound, each team has to pass their beach ball from one player to the next by hitting it with their hand like in volleyball. If a player catches the ball or the ball hits the ground, that team loses that round. The team that keeps the ball airborne the longest wins the round, and the team that wins 3 out of 5 or 4 out of 7 rounds wins the game.

This game is more fun when it's played with 3 to 5 teams of 5 to 6 players each.

Ring Toss

Materials Needed: 10 quarter-inch wooden dowels used by everybody; paper plates with their centers cut out, about a dozen for each player.

Players: Individuals compete against each other or have teams of 2 or more players each.

How It's Played: This is like the old carnival game. Each player or team gets the same number of cut-out paper plate "rings." Standing at a designated spot behind a chalk or tape line, players have to fling their plates and get them on the wooden dowels that are stuck in the ground about twelve inches apart and 5 to 8 feet away. The team that gets the most ringers in 3 minutes wins. Make sure each team has their own plate color or marking.

If the game is played indoors, the wooden dowels can be cut short and stuck vertically into a wide flat cardboard box or they can be taped to the front of a long table with gaffer's tape, which can be bought in a hardware store.

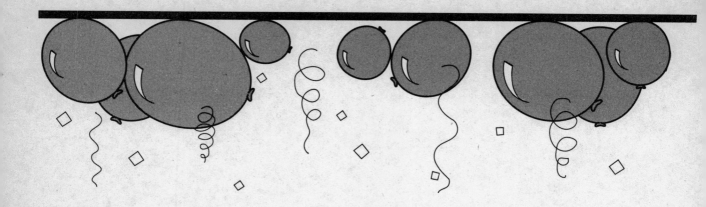

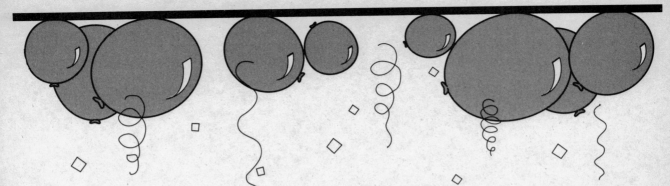

Wet and
Messy
Fun
Games

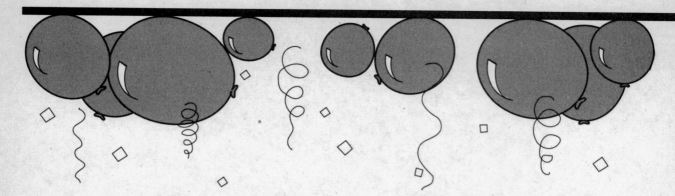

Water Waiter Relay

Materials for Each Team: Two dozen large paper cups (12 full and 12 empty), a pitcher of colored water, 2 tables or chairs, and a tray hat for each player.

Players: Teams of 2 or more players each.

How It's Played: Set up 2 tables or chairs about 16 to 18 feet apart. Put a piece of tape on the floor to mark the halfway point. One chair holds a dozen paper cups filled with water, a dozen empty cups and the pitcher of water. All the players must wear tray hats. One player stands by the chair that has the cups filled with water and the other player from that team stands on the halfway mark.

At the starting sound, the player next to the cups of water has to pick one up, place it on top of their tray hat, walk as fast as they can to the player on the halfway mark, and transfer the cup to that player's tray hat, who then goes to the empty chair and deposits the cup. The first team to transport one dozen cups from one chair to the other wins.

If a cup spills, the player at the first chair has to get another cup and begin again at the starting line. If the team runs out of cups of water it is also that first player's job to fill more cups.

For every additional player on a team, add another relay position by placing an additional mark on the floor between the 2 chairs.

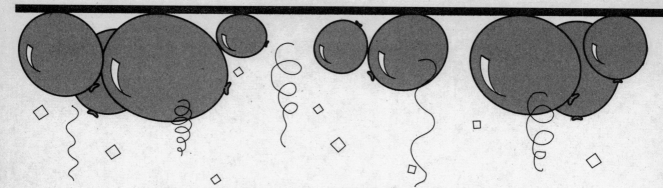

Two Hands Aren't Better than One

Materials for Each Team: A cup, a box with 10 pounds of flour, sugar or sand in it, an empty box the same size, and 2 blindfolds.

Players: Teams with no more than 2 players each.

How It's Played: This game can be played on a table or on the floor. 2 blindfolded players stand at a table side by side. The right-hand wrist of one player is tied to the left-hand wrist ofthe other player, and together they hold a small cup. On the table is a box of flour and an empty box, about 2 feet away. At the starting sound, the teammates have to scoop flour out of one box and pour it into the empty box as fast as they can. The team that transfers the most flour in the allotted time of 2 to 3 minutes wins.

The transferred flour can be measured with a ruler or use a box with inch increments marked off on the inside as the receiving receptacle.

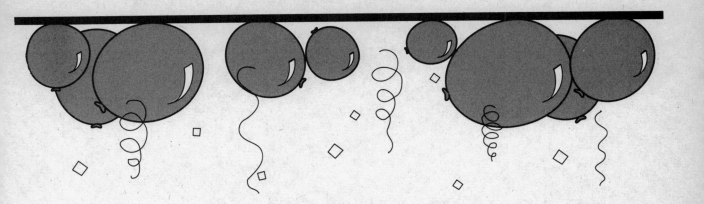

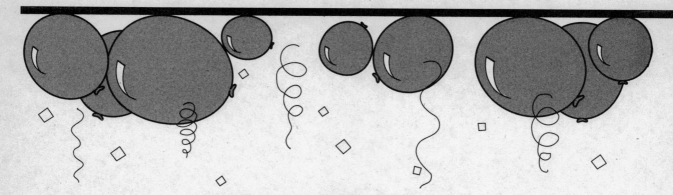

Egg Heads

Materials for Each Team: A bucket with 12 eggs, an empty bucket, and a plastic sheet for the floor.

Players: Teams of 2 or more players each. (Teams need to have an even number of players.)

How It's Played: With tape or chalk mark off start and finish lines about 15 feet apart. On the starting line, place a bowl of 6 eggs and at the finish line put an empty bowl.

Standing behind the starting line, 2 players from a team bend their heads towards each other and place an egg there, so that it is balanced between their heads. At the starting sound, they make their way to the finish line as fast as they can and, still using their heads, gently drop the egg into the empty bowl, so it doesn't break. If it breaks, they go back for another one.

The first team to transport 6 eggs from start to finish wins. If you want to add more players to a team, make it a relay; have the first 2 players carry the egg ten feet and pass it with their hands to 2 more players, who have to take it another 10 feet to the empty bowl. With this formula, you can add as many players as you like, as long as it's an even number.

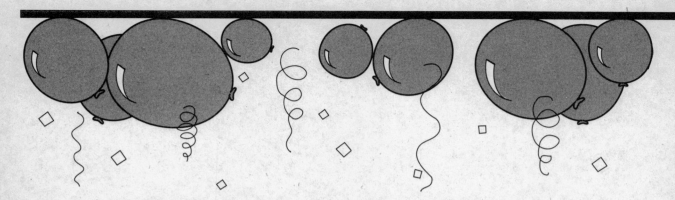

Help! There's a Hole in My Funnel

Materials for Each Team: A plastic drop cloth for quick cleanup, 2 chairs, one empty box and one box filled with at least ten pounds of sandbox sand (it's cleaner and finer than other types of sand), and a small funnel for each player.

Players: Teams of 2 or 3 players each.

How It's Played: With tape or chalk mark 2 lines on the floor, about 10 feet apart. Set up chairs behind each mark. On the chairs at the starting line, place the boxes filled with sand, one for each team. (Boxes can also be placed on the floor.) On the other chairs, place the empty boxes.

The teams start behind the starting line. At the starting sound, they fill their funnels with sand and run to their empty box ten feet away, letting the sand spill out as they run. What's left in the funnel they dump in the box, then run back for more. The process continues until time is up.

The team with the most sand in their receiving box at the end of the allotted time of 3 minutes wins. (The faster they run between boxes the less they'll lose.)

Make sure the receiving boxes have inch increments marked off on the inside so you can tell how much sand has been collected.

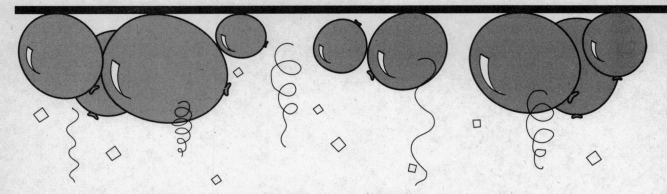

Oops! You Missed

Materials for Each Player: A large bowl of colored water, a cup, a container hat, a plastic drop cloth for quick cleanup, and large plastic trash bags with holes cut out for arms and heads, to keep the players dry.

Players: Individuals play against each other.

How It's Played: Each player wears a container hat and has a bowl of water.

At the starting sound, the players, using only one hand, have to scoop up water from their bowls with their cups and put it into the container hats on top of their heads. Because they won't be able to see what they're doing, water will fall all over them, causing a lot of wet excitement.

The player that gets the most water into the container by the end of the allotted time wins. Measure the depth of the water with a ruler.

Use popcorn if you want to keep the game dry, but water is a lot more fun. For real slime-hungry players, use colored corn syrup, but make sure you have damp towels ready for quick cleanup.

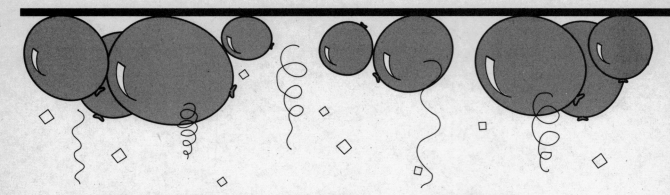

Mile-High Whipped-Cream Sandwich

Materials for Each Team: A tray hat, 2 cans of whipped cream, 12 pieces of bread, and a chair.

Players: Teams of 3 players each.

How It's Played: One player sits in a chair wearing the tray hat. The other teammates stand on either side, one with a can of whipped cream and the other with the slices of bread (square pieces of corrugated cardboard can be substituted).

At the starting sound, each team has to build the tallest whipped-cream sandwich possible on top of their teammate's tray hat. One player puts down a layer of whipped cream and the other tops it off with a slice of bread.

The team with the tallest sandwich in the allotted time of three minutes wins. To make it more daring and exciting, don't use the tray hats and make the sandwiches right on top of the head.

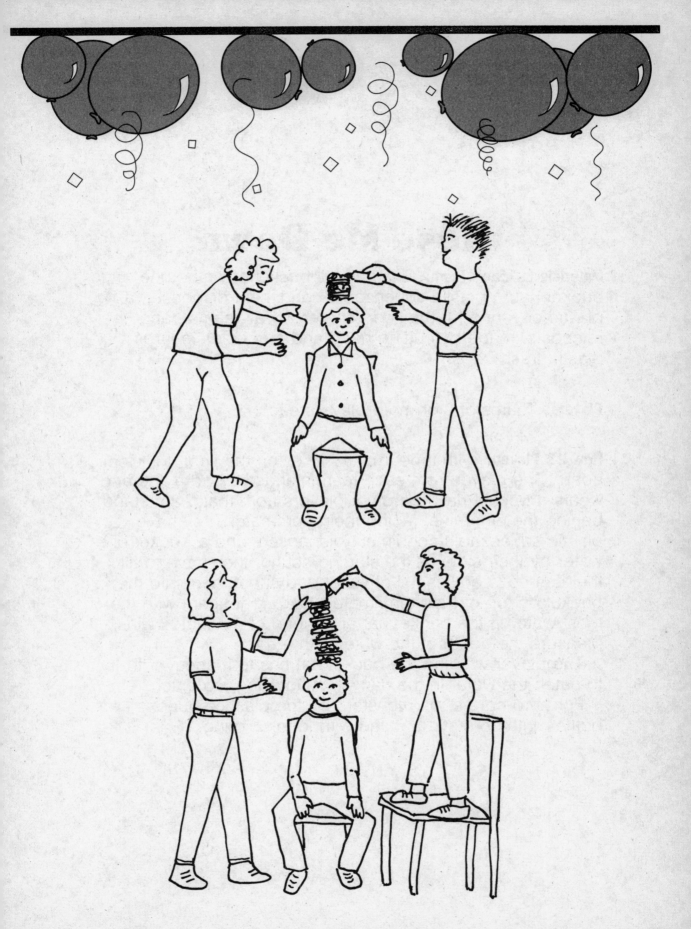

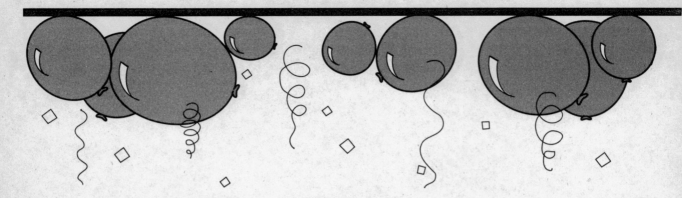

Hose Me Down

Materials for Each Team: One half full bucket of water, one bucket hat, a plastic squeezable condiment dispenser, a plastic covering for the floor (shared by all teams), and raincoats, made by cutting head and arm holes in large plastic trash bags.

Players: Teams of 2 or more players each.

How It's Played: With tape, make 2 lines on the floor, four feet apart. One player from each team stands behind a line and wears a bucket hat. The other players from that team stand behind the other line, facing their teammate. They have plastic squeezable condiment dispensers and a bucket of water by their side. At the starting sound, they have to fill their squeeze bottles full of water and shoot them into the bucket on top of their teammate's head. The team with the most water in the bucket hat at the end of 4 minutes wins. Measure the depth of the water with a ruler.

The player wearing the bucket hat has to maneuver to try to catch the water in the hat without spilling too much.

For hard-core slime monsters, fill the plastic squeeze bottles with corn syrup tinted with food coloring.

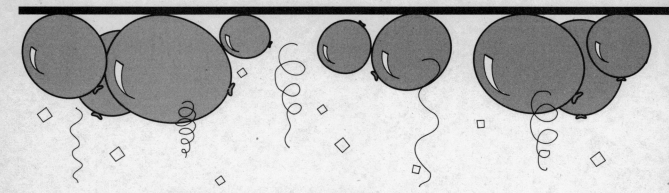

Mummy Masters

Materials for Each Team: A bucket of water, 2 sponges, 2 rolls of toilet paper, and a painters' disposable paper jumpsuit which can be brought in a paintstore.

Players: Teams of 2 or 3 players each.

How It's Played: At the starting sound, one player stands up straight. The other two players have to mummify their teammate by covering them from neck to toe with toilet paper (except for the arms, which can remain free). The first team to complete this task wins. (Make sure the players being mummified are approximately the same size and height.)

The wrappers should use sponges to dampen the outside of the mummy's jumpsuit so that the toilet paper will stick. (Suggestion: Have one player dampen the immediate area to be mummified, starting at the bottom or the top, as the other player carefully unravels the toilet paper around the mummy, covering every inch.

Remember, the mummy has to be completely covered, except for their head and arms. Nothing underneath can show through. A referee will be needed to make a final judgment.

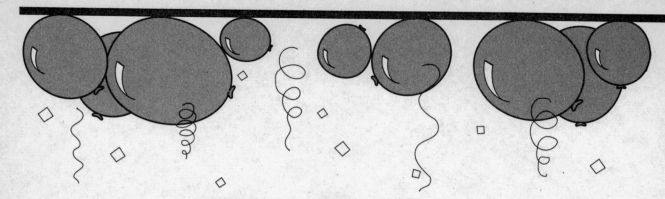

Elbow Fishing

Materials for Each Player: 24 large hard candies (make sure you can pick them up with your elbows) and a box or bowl a player can fit their elbows into, and shaving cream or Jell-O.

Players: Teams of 3 or more players each. Individuals can also play against each other.

How It's Played: Each player gets a big bowl or 1 x 1 foot plastic-lined box filled with shaving cream or jello. Hidden inside are twenty-four hard candies.

At the starting sound, the players have to dig through the goop, only using their elbows, as fast as they can to extract all the candies. The first player or team of players to do this wins, or whoever finds the most candies in 3 minutes wins.

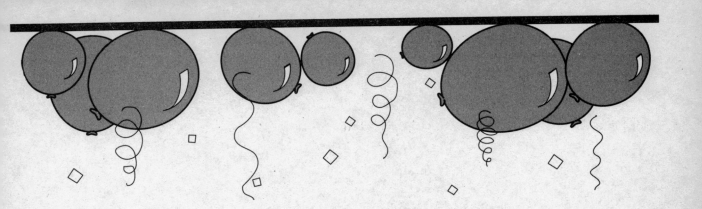

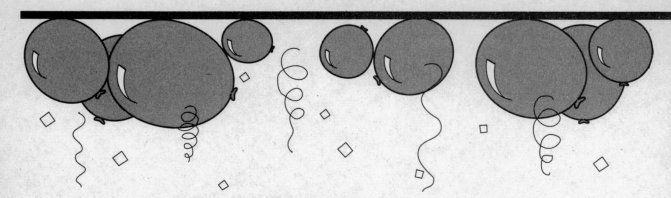

The Big Squeeze

Materials for Each Player on a Team: A cardboard painter's bucket (which can be found at a home improvement center, paint or hardware store) and a large sponge. Put a plastic sheet on the floor for quick cleanup.

Players: Teams of 4 or more. (It must be an even number.)

How It's Played: With tape or chalk mark off 3 lines on the floor, 6 feet apart. One players stands on the first line with a bucket of water and a large sponge. The second and third players on spot number two have an empty bucket, and the fourth player from the team, who is on spot number three, also has an empty bucket.

At the starting sound, the player on the first mark dunks a sponge in the bucket of water and throws it to player number two on the second mark, who squeezes out the sponge into the empty pail. Player number 3, who is also on the second mark, soaks the water back up in the sponge and throws it to player four on the third mark, who squeezes out the sponge into that empty bucket. The first team to transfer all their water from the first mark to the third mark wins.

For every 2 additional players on a team, add another relay spot down the line.

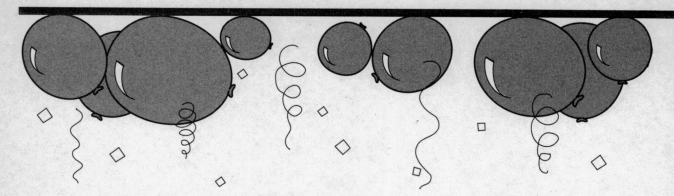

In Your Face

Materials for Each Team: 26, 8½ x 11 sheets of paper, a pie plate partially filled with molasses, a waterproof marker, and damp towels for quick post-game cleanup.

Players: Teams of 2 to 5 players each.

How It's Played: On the floor mark off start and finish lines ten feet apart, using tape or chalk. Behind the starting line each team has their pile of 26 sheets of paper. Each sheet has a different letter of the alphabet on it, written big and bold with the waterproof marker. Next to that is a disposable pie plate partially filled with molasses.

At the starting sound the players, one at a time, have to dip their cheeks in the molasses. When they are all sticky they go to the alphabet pile and pick up a letter, with their cheek (no hands), run across the finish line as fast as they can, and deposit the letter in a pile in alphabetical order using only their elbows to get the paper sheet off.

The first team to transfer the entire alphabet over the finish line wins. If a letter is out of order, the second-place team wins by default.

Note: If a player's cheek remains sticky enough to pick up additional letters, they don't have to keep dunking it in the molasses.

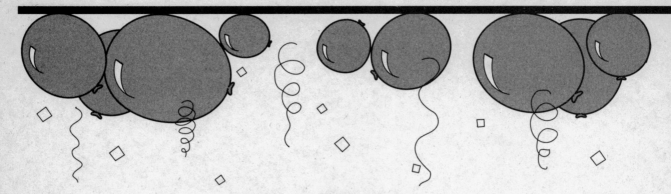

Egg Holes

Materials for Each Team: A dozen eggs, a 2 x 4 foot piece of sturdy cardboard, and a plastic drop cloth for the floor.

Players: Teams of two players each.

How It's Played: Cut a dozen, random 3-inch wide holes into each team's piece of cardboard. (When preparing the game, try to find the flattest piece of cardboard possible. An adult should cut out the holes with a mat knife.

Each team holds their board, one player on each end. At the starting sound, one player puts an egg on the edge of the board and both players, by tilting and maneuvering, try to get the egg from one end of the board to the other as fast as they can without it falling through the holes. The first team to get 4 eggs across are the winners (or the team to get the most across in the allotted time of 5 minutes wins). If an egg breaks, a fresh one is picked up and placed at the beginning.

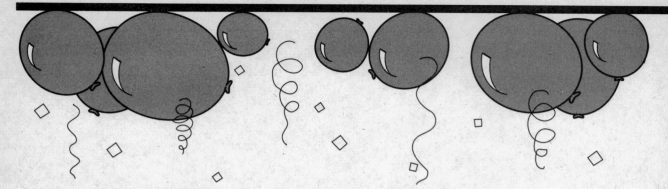

Popcorn Sprint

Materials for Each Team: 2 buckets, or cardboard boxes, a jumbo bag of popcorn, and a pair of sneakers with a plastic cup taped over each toe. (See diagram to the right, below.)

Players: Teams of 3 players each.

How It's Played: Using 2 strips of white or colored tape, mark off start and finish lines 10 or 15 feet apart, place an empty bucket at the starting line and a popcorn-filled bucket at the finish line.

One player sits by the popcorn bucket and the two other players wear cup sneakers and stand by the empty bucket. At the starting sound, the players with the cup sneakers have to run across the finish line to their teammate, who fills their foot cups with popcorn. They run back to the empty bucket at the starting line and, by using only their feet, empty their popcorn into the empty bucket. This process continues until all the popcorn is transferred from one bucket to the other. The team that transfers the most popcorn in the allotted time of 4 minutes wins. A ruler can be used to measure the depth of each team's popcorn at the end of the challenge.

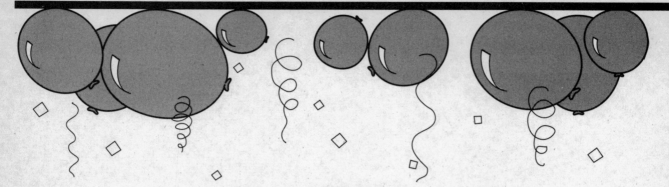

Egg-a-Thon

Materials for Each Player: 6 eggs, a flat-top hat, and a plastic sheet to cover the floor for quick cleanup.

Players: Teams of 3 or more players each.

How It's Played: Team players all wear flat-top hats and stand in a line, one behind the other. At the starting sound, the first person in line places an egg in the center of their flat-top hat. The challenge is for players to tilt their heads forward just enough so that the egg rolls down to the edge and onto the hat of the next player in front of them. The second player has to bend back to receive the egg, then tilt forward to pass the egg on to the third player. This is done until the last person in line receives the egg, leans forward, catches the egg and puts it in a bowl. The first team that gets the egg all the way down the line wins. (To lengthen the game, play for 3 out of 5 rounds.)

Since every player is facing forward, and is not allowed to turn to see the egg coming from behind, their teammates can give them directions: "Tilt your head to the left, tilt your head to the right, move down a little bit." If an egg breaks en route, the first person in line picks up another egg and starts the process at the beginning of the line.

This game is for older players—12 and up.

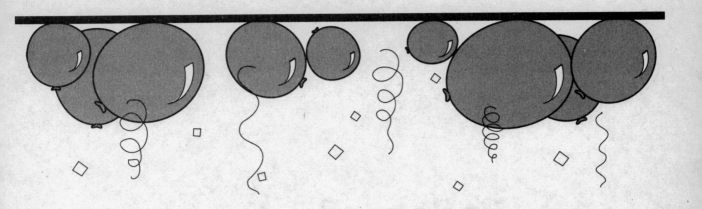

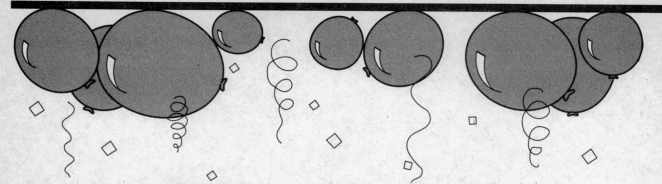

Balloon Busters

Materials for Each Player: A painter's paper jumpsuit, 15 balloons, a can of whipped cream, gaffer's tape, (which can be bought in a hardware store), blankets, and a plastic sheet for the floor.

Players: Individual players compete against each other, or have teams.

How It's Played: Each player wears a paper jumpsuit covered with balloons that are filled with whipped cream. Tape the balloons to the suit with gaffer's tape. At the starting sound, players try to break their balloons as fast as possible by rolling around on the floor without using their hands. The player that breaks all the balloons first wins. (If teams are competing, the team whose players break the most balloons in the allotted time of 4 minutes wins.)

This game should be played on an area covered with blankets, so when the kids roll around on the floor they won't get hurt.

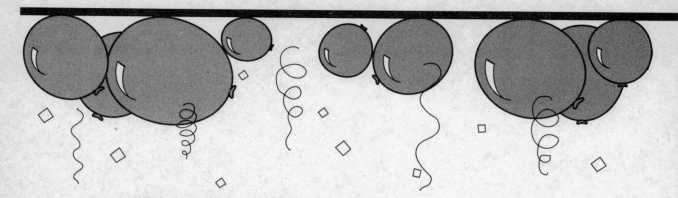

Exploding Tomatoes

Materials for Each Team: Tomatoes, a blindfold, a plastic covering for the floor and a pair of swimming flippers. (If flippers aren't available, tape a 12 x 12 inch piece of corrugated cardboard with plastic packaging tape to the bottom of each sneaker. See diagram below)

Players: Teams of 2 players each.

How It's Played: For each team, mark off an area with tape or chalk about 5 feet wide and 10 feet long. Place tomatoes randomly, about 1½ to 2 feet apart, over the entire area. At the starting sound a player wearing flippers walks down the track blindfolded. The object is to walk through without crushing any tomatoes. To accomplish this, the player's teammate stands outside of the track and gives directions on how to avoid stepping on the tomatoes. The team that makes it down the track and back three times and squashes the fewest tomatoes wins. (Eggs or small paper cups of water can also be used.)

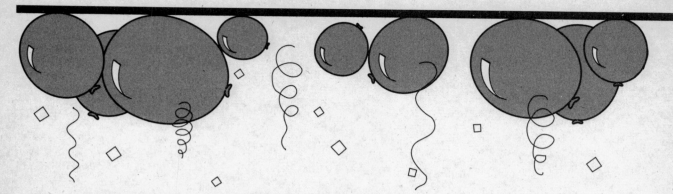

Human Whipped-Cream Pie

Materials for Each Team: 4 cans of whipped cream, a cherry, a plastic sheet on the floor, a change of clothing or plastic trash bags with holes cut out for head, arms, and legs, or raincoats, and damp towels for post-game cleanup.

Players: Teams of 2 or 3 players each.

How It's Played: Each team is equipped with 4 cans of whipped cream. One member of the team has to lie on the floor face up. At the starting sound, the other players have to cover their teammate from neck to foot with whipped cream and then place a cherry on the forehead for fun. To make it even more messy, have them add a can of chocolate sauce before they add the cherry. The first team to complete the task wins.

Remember, every inch of the person's body, except the head, has to be covered in whipped cream, so a referee will be needed. When the contest is over the plastic sheet will be very slippery so be careful and remove it quickly.

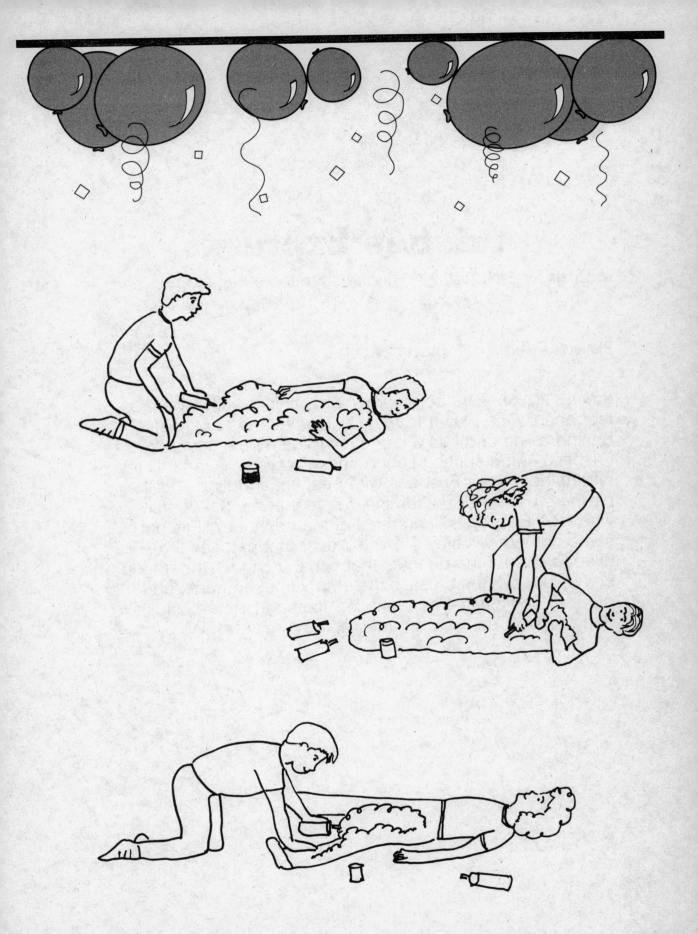

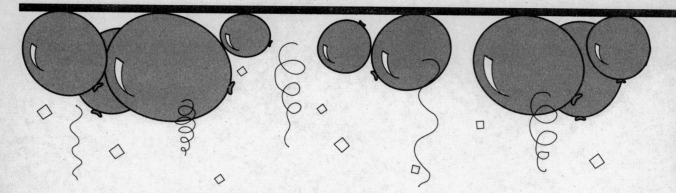

Frisbee Express

Materials for Each Team: A Frisbee, styrofoam packaging peanuts, and a bucket.

Players: Teams of 2 players each.

How It's Played: For each team, mark off lines with tape, 10 feet apart. One player from each team stands or kneels behind a line and has a box of styrofoam peanuts and a Frisbee. At the starting sound, these players have to fill the underside of their Frisbees with peanuts and fling it to their partners behind the other line, ten feet away. (Of course when the Frisbee is flung most of the peanuts will fly out, but some of them will stay in.) The player that catches the Frisbee dumps the peanuts that come along for the ride in a box or bucket, then tosses the empty Frisbee back, and the process continues. The team that transports the most peanuts from one side to the other in 4 minutes wins.

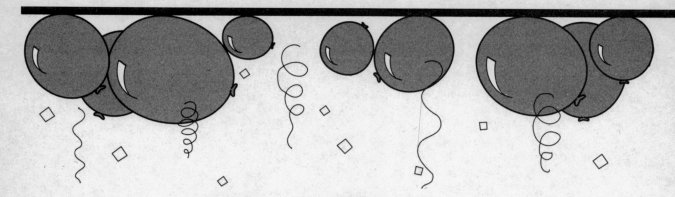

Pong Derby

Materials for Each Player: A large squirt gun, a bowl of water for refilling, 6 ping-pong balls, and a plastic sheet for the floor.

Players: Individuals play against each other, or have teams of 2 or more players each.

How It's Played: Set up start and finish lines with tape or chalk, 15 or more feet apart. On the starting line set up 6 ping-pong balls. At the starting sound, a player has to shoot the balls over the finish line with a squirt gun, then down the track, back over the starting line, and then over the finish line again. (If teams are playing, make sure there are at least two balls per player.)

There should be enough distance between each team's track so there is no chance of balls straying. Mark each team's balls with a different color or a special marking to avoid mix-ups.

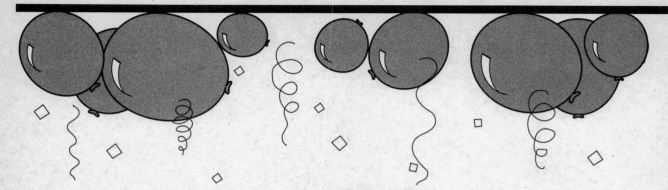

Scrambled Eggs

Materials for Each Team: 6 eggs and a top sheet for a twin bed (or 2½ yards from a bolt of inexpensive fabric), and a blindfold.

Players: Teams of 3 players each.

How It's Played: An egg is put in the center of a sheet. One player from a team holds one end of the sheet. Their teammate stands on a taped mark, on the outside, near the center of the sheet and holds a plastic baseball bat, ready to smash the egg. The sheet holder gives the batter directions to help make contact. Simultaneously, a player from another team holds the other end of the sheet and moves it up and down, making sure the egg never stays in one place and hoping the batter never hits it.

   At the starting sound, it's egg smashing time. Once an egg is smashed, the team puts another egg on the sheet. The first team to smash 6 eggs wins or the team that smashes the most eggs in 4 minutes wins.

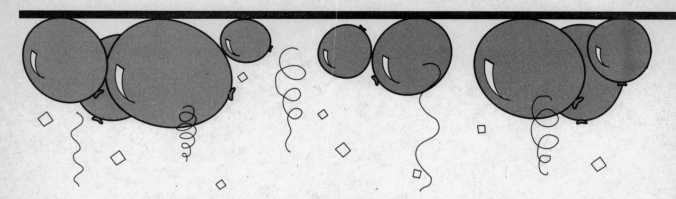

Sundae Mountain

Materials for Each Team: A large plate or pan for each team's sundae and an ice cream scoop for each player. A half-dozen pints of different flavors of ice cream (to be shared between two teams sitting across from each other), 2 cans of whipped cream, 2 jars of chocolate sauce, and assorted toppings, which could include chopped nuts, sprinkles, Reese's Pieces, M&M's.

Players: Teams of 2 or more players each, or have individuals play against each other.

How It's Played: The team that builds the tallest ice cream sundae in a five-minute period wins. This will take some strategy. With a can of whipped cream alone you can make a foot-high mound.

When the contest is over, everyone can have fun eating their ice cream creations.

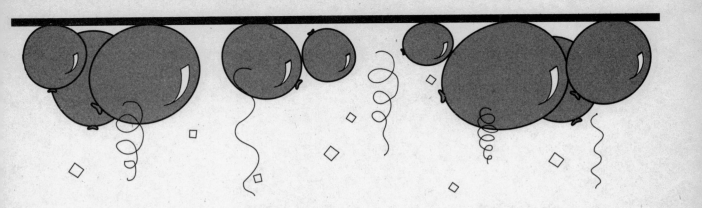

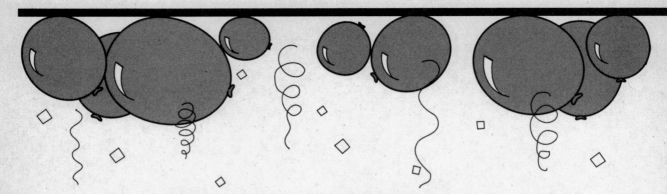

Shaving the Floor

Materials for Each Player: A disposable razor (take the blade out or cover it with tape), shaving cream or whipped cream, a large bowl of water, and a plastic drop cloth for the floor.

Players: Individuals compete against each other, or have teams of 2 or more players each.

How It's Played: Each team starts out with an area on the floor, at least 3 x 3 feet, that is covered with shaving cream. The more players on a team, the bigger the area should be. (Make sure the same amount of shaving cream is used on each area.)

At the starting sound, players start shaving. The challenge is to be the first team to shave the shaving cream off their area. Each teams gets a bowl of water to rinse their razors in between strokes.

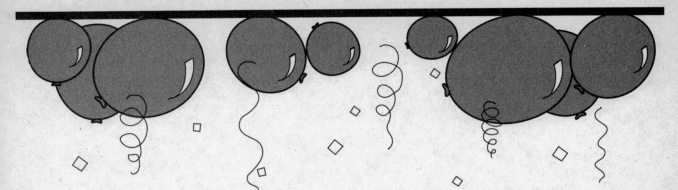

Brain
Games

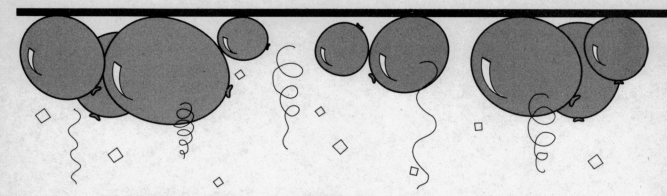

Reading, Writing, and Toemanship

Materials for Each Player: A marker that can be held between the toes and pieces of paper.

Players: Individuals compete against each other, or have teams of 2 or more players each.

How It's Played: Each player get a marker that will fit between their toes and several pieces of paper. Players use one foot to hold down the paper and the other foot to do the writing. The host asks a question about a subject that's appropriate for the age of the kids playing, like popular music, TV shows, movies, science, history, and math.

The first player to write out the correct answer with their foot yells out "I've got it!" If the answer is correct, that player wins that round for the team. If the answer is wrong, the round continues until someone gets the right answer. Play for the best of 4 out of 7 rounds.

The game master should decide from the onset of the game whether or not spelling counts.

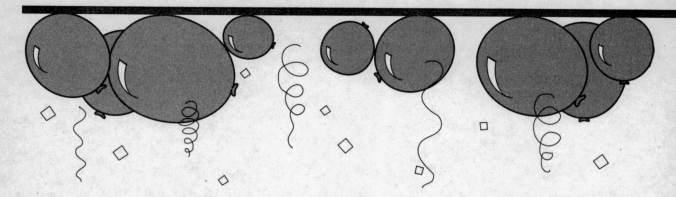

Mystery Sounds

Materials Needed: A portable cassette recorder and a cassette tape of 3-second bits of recorded household sounds and/or theme music from favorite kid shows or musical groups.

Players: 2 or more teams of 2 or 3 players each.

How It's Played: In preparation for the game, the game master records sound bits from TV shows, rock groups, and sounds around the house, like the dog eating, someone snoring, rain, or water draining from the bathtub.

The game master plays a sound. If a player recognizes it, the teammates confer, and if they agree, then the player raises a hand—as fast as possible. If players from both teams raise their hands at the same time then neither team gets any points. If one team player raises a hand first and gets the answer right, that team gets 10 points. If the answer is wrong, 10 points goes to the opposing team. The team with the most points after all the sounds have been heard wins.

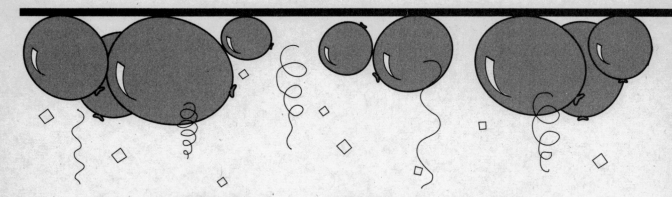

Tower of Power

Materials for Each Team: Two dozen square pieces of stiff cardboard no larger than a foot in any one direction and several rolls of tape.

Players: Single players can play against each other, or have teams of 2 or more players each.

How It's Played: Each team gets a pile of square pieces of cardboard and lots of tape. At the starting sound, they begin building the tallest structure possible. The team or player that does this in the allotted time wins. A captain should be appointed for each team to guide the construction.

Players are going to need at least 10 minutes for this game. To make it more fun play everyone's favorite music while they're building.

This game is for kids 9 to 12 years old.

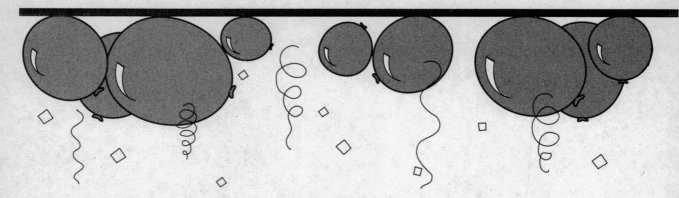

Secret Objects

Materials Needed: Names of common objects written on separate pieces of paper, like bicycle, tree, mailbox.

Players: Teams of 2 to 4 people each.

How It's Played: The game master gives one player from each team a piece of paper with the name of a common item written on it. (Each player gets the same word.) Those players stand up in front of their teammates, who have to ask questions to guess what the object is. The holder of the secret word can only answer "yes" or "no". All the teams can play at the same time and hear all the other questions and guesses that are shouted out.

10 points is given to the first team that figures out the secret object. The team with the most points at the end of the allotted time of 7 minutes wins, or the first team that wins 2 out of 3 or 3 out of 5 rounds wins. For each new round a different team player is the keeper of the secret word.

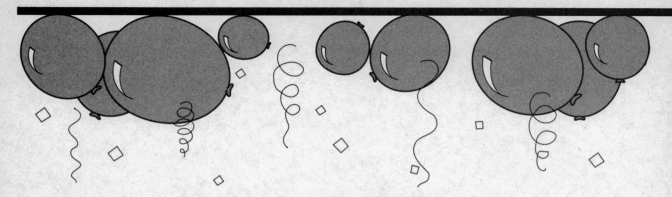

Tic, Tac, What?

Materials Needed: A large piece of poster board for every 2 players, markers, and a set of trivia questions and answers.

Players: 2 teams of 2 or more players each. (There must be an even number.)

How It's Played: To prepare, draw large extended tic-tac-toe grids, with 16 squares instead of 9, on large pieces of poster board or paper and tape them to a wall. One team is the "X's" and the other the "O's" (which will be decided by a flip of a coin by the referee). One player from each team shares a grid and competes in a game of tic-tac-toe. The game starts when a coin is flipped to see which team goes first. The referee asks that team a question and if one of the players from that team thinks they know the answer, they call it out. If they're right, they get to make their team's mark in a square on their grid. If the answer is wrong of if they don't know the answer, the question goes to the other team. If nobody knows the answer, a new question is picked. If both teams yell out the correct answer at the same time, they both score. When a team gets a right answer, the next question goes to the opposing team.

The challenge is to be the first team to fill in a row either across, down, or diagonally on one of the grids. If it takes too long for either team to win a grid, then the team with the most "X's" or "O's" within an allotted time wins.

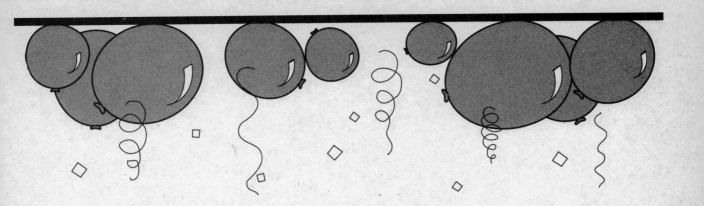

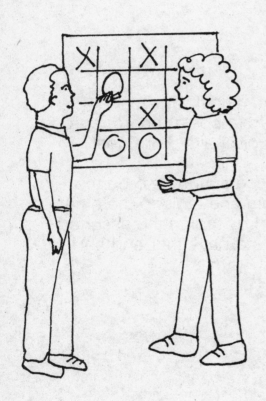

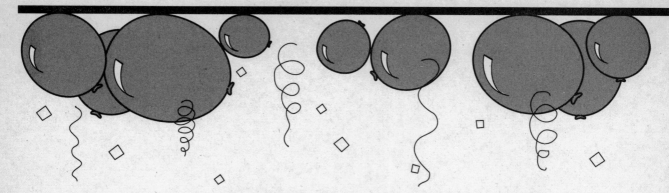

Bridge It

Materials for Each Team: 2 tables or chairs, a roll of tape for each player, and several sheets of poster board cut in different shapes.

Players: Teams of 2 to 4 players.

How It's Played: Each player or team starts out with an identical pile of different shapes cut from poster board, and a roll of scotch tape. Set up 2 tables or chairs 5 or 6 feet apart.

   The object of the game at the starting sound is to be the first team to make a bridge going from one table to the other (or the back of one chair to the other) by taping the assorted shapes together. Teammates should start at either end and meet in the middle.

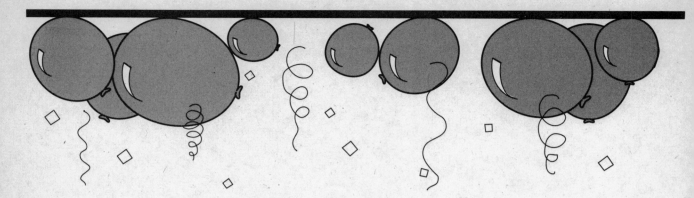

Bollix

Materials Needed: A wide nibbed black marker and a large sheet of poster board for each team, or a blackboard shared by all the teams. Flash cards for the game master. (Use a 12 x 12 inch piece of white poster board or bigger and a wide nibbed black marker to write the words.)

Players: Individuals compete, or have 3 or more teams of no more than 2 players each.

How It's Played: The challenge starts with the game master showing all the teams a flash card for 10 seconds. The card has 4 simple words written on it in a vertical row. At the starting sound, the players go to the blackboard and one player from each team writes down the words in the correct order after conferring with their teammates. (Spelling counts.) Those who write the words down in the wrong order or make a spelling mistake sit down, but their teammates remain standing. If everyone gets it right they all continue playing.

The game master then flashes another card with 3 of the old words and one new one, written in a new order. The players left standing again write down the words in a vertical column, in the correct order. This process of remixing the words and replacing one with a new word continues until there is a winning team or player left standing.

If only a few teams are competing or teams are eliminated quickly you can play for 3 out of 5 rounds or whatever seems appropriate.

Note: Use simple words that have 2 to 5 letters.

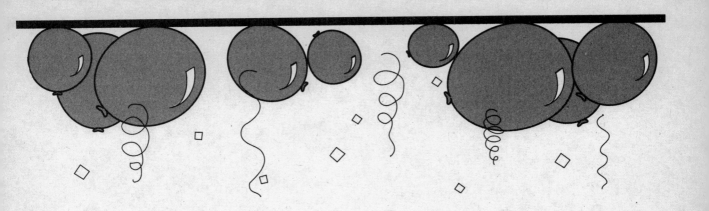

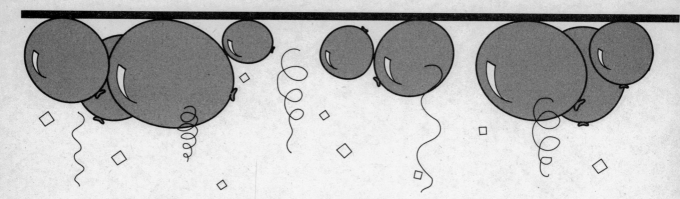

Scrabble Scramble

Materials to Prepare the Game: A list of words appropriate for the age group playing, a wide-tipped marker, and letters of the alphabet written individually on single sheets of paper or poster board.

Players: Individuals play against each other, or have teams of 2 players each.

How It's Played: The referee yells out a word and each team or player has to spell the word using the giant letters. The first team or player to do so raises their hands, and if they are correct, they get 10 points. The first team or player to get seventy points wins.

If a team raises their hands and they have misspelled the word, the opposing team gets 10 points. If both teams raise their hands at the same time and both have the correct answer, then both teams score.

How to Prepare the Letters: Using small pieces of white poster board or 8½ x 11 inch paper, print the letters of the alphabet, one capital letter per sheet, using a wide-tipped black marker. Make the letters big and bold so everyone in the playing area can see them. Make sure that each team or player has more than enough letters in their pile to spell the words you pick for the game.

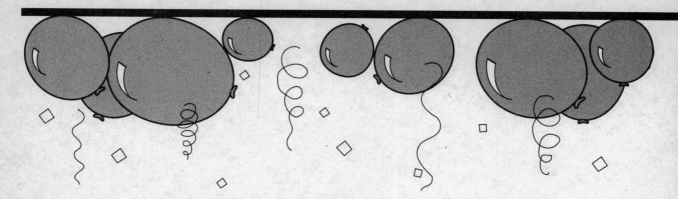

Giant Jigsaw

Materials Needed: A pencil, masking tape, a wide-tipped marker, poster board, and a utility knife (which should only be used by an adult).

Players: Individuals play against each other, or have teams of two or more players.

How It's Played: Each player or team gets identical jigsaw puzzles. The object of the game at the starting sound, is to be the first to complete the puzzle.

HOW TO MAKE SEVERAL SETS OF IDENTICAL SHAPES CUT FROM POSTER BOARD

Tape 2 sheets of poster board together on the longest edge; put tape only on one side and lay the taped side face down. Now tape 2 more pieces together on the longest edge and place it tape side down on top of the first, so one set is directly on top of the other. Tape the edges together in a couple of places with small pieces of tape so they don't slide around.

With a pencil, lightly sketch out your shapes, (use your imagination), just make sure the shapes are 6 to 10 inches across. Once you are happy with your design, go over it with a wide-tipped black marker once or twice so the lines are nice and thick. Place your 2 taped-together boards on a cutting board and, using a utility knife (only used by an adult) or scissors, cut out your puzzle pieces by following the black marker lines.

If it's too difficult to cut through 2 boards at the same time,

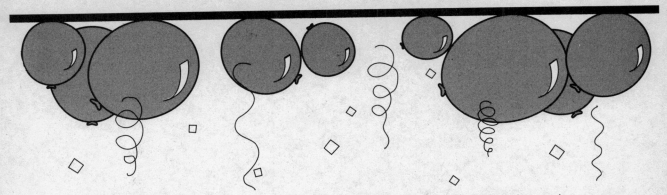

cut through one, then use those pieces as a template, by tracing their shapes on the next boards. Follow this same procedure for each additional set you need.

Keep each set of shapes in separate bags or boxes until the game is ready to be played.

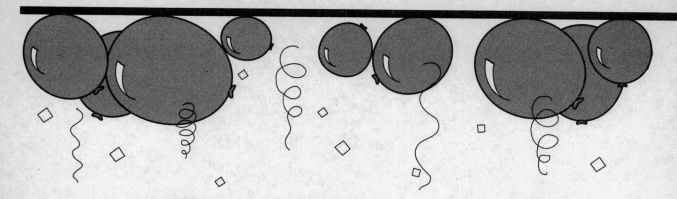

Simple Charades

Materials for Both Teams: A list of simple actions which can be acted out in charades. Sitting in a chair, riding a bicycle, driving a car, playing football, skiing, are some examples.

Players: 2 teams of 3 or more players each.

How It's Played: Pick one player from each team who likes to perform to act out the actions (one at a time) in front of both teams. The referee flips a coin to decide which pantomimist goes first. Players from both teams yell out the answers until a team gets one right. Then it's the other team's pantomimist who acts out the next action. Each correct answer is worth ten points. If both teams yell out the correct answer at the same time, they both score. The first team to score 100 points wins.

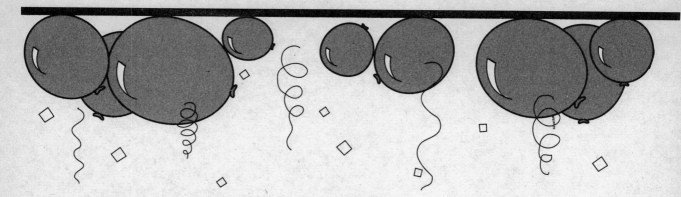

Lightning Round

Materials Needed: A stopwatch for the referee and a list of categories. Pick ones that kids like and know a lot about: TV shows, names of states, movie titles, rock groups, names of foods, science and geography questions, etc.

Players: Individuals can play against each other, but it is more fun when you have 2 teams of at least five or more players each who are 12 years or older.

How It's Played: The game master flips a coin to see which team goes first. At the starting sound, one player at a time, going from left to right, has only five seconds to name one item in the chosen category. (Time it with a stopwatch.) As soon as the first player responds, the clock is on for the second player, and so on, all the way down the line until each player from a team gets a chance. If a player gives an incorrect answer, is stumped, or doesn't respond within 5 seconds, they leave the game. After each team has had a shot at a category, a new category is picked. The team with the most players left at the end of the allotted time (about 7 minutes) wins. To lengthen the game, play for the best of 3 out of 5 rounds.

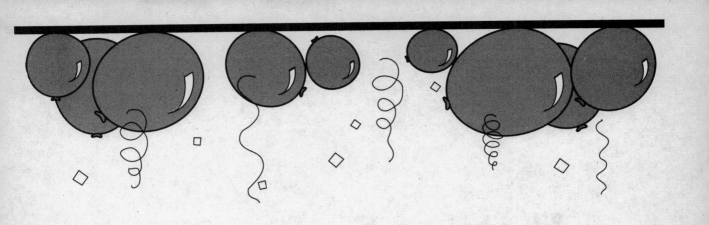

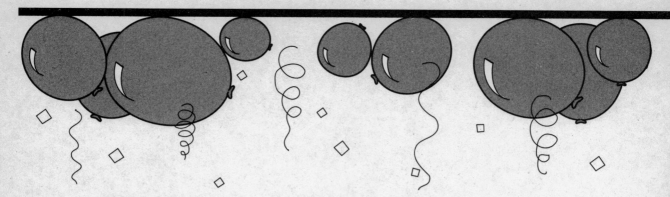

There's a Spelling Bee
in My Soup

Materials for Each Player: A sheet of paper, a bowl of alphabet soup or alphabet cereal in milk, and a spoon. This can be played on a table or a floor with a plastic sheet on it.

Players: Individual players compete against each other.

How It's Played: At the starting sound, players start picking out letters from their soup or cereal. The challenge is for them to spell out words on the pieces of paper by their bowls. The player that spells the most words in 5 minutes wins.

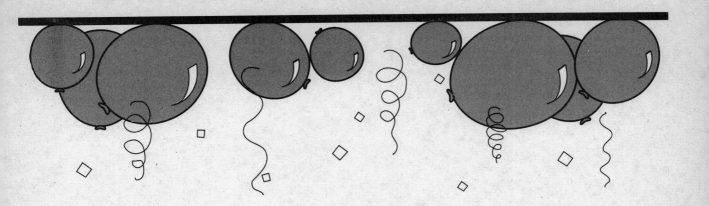

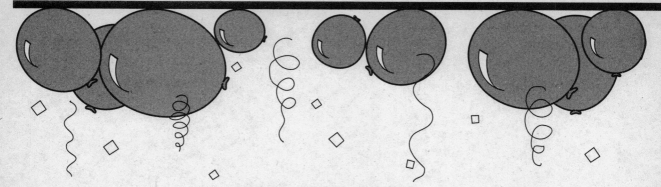

Dots All

Materials for Each Team: A wide-tipped marker and 4 or more simple connect-the-dot patterns.

Players: Individual players compete against each other.

How It's Played: Each player gets an identical set of four connect-the-dot patterns. At the starting sound, players start connecting the dots as fast as they can. The object of the game is to be the first to identify the pictures by writing the name of the picture below the pattern.

How to Prepare the Dot Patterns: Make up your own or copy the ones on the following page onto large sheets of white poster board. Use one pattern per board. Lightly pencil in numbers on the poster board, then connect them lightly with the pencil to make sure they are positioned correctly. Once the positions are correct, go over the numbers with a wide-tipped black marker and erase your pencil connections.

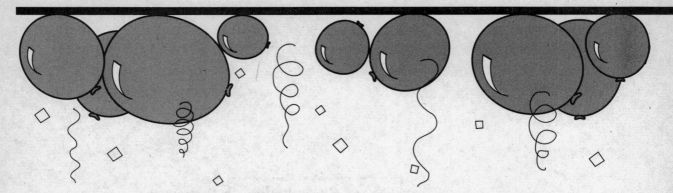

Like Tubular Man

Materials for Each Team: Assorted shapes 6 to 12 inches wide in any direction that are cut from poster board, scotch tape, and a golf ball–sized ball.

Players: Teams of 3 or 4 players each.

How It's Played: At the starting sound, each team has to use the scraps of poster board and scotch tape to build a cardboard tunnel 4 feet long and wide enough to pass the ball through. (A strip of tape placed on the floor by the game master can be used as a guide for length.)

The challenge is to be the first team to construct a tunnel and pass the ball through and out the other end. Make sure there are more than enough pieces of poster board for each team.

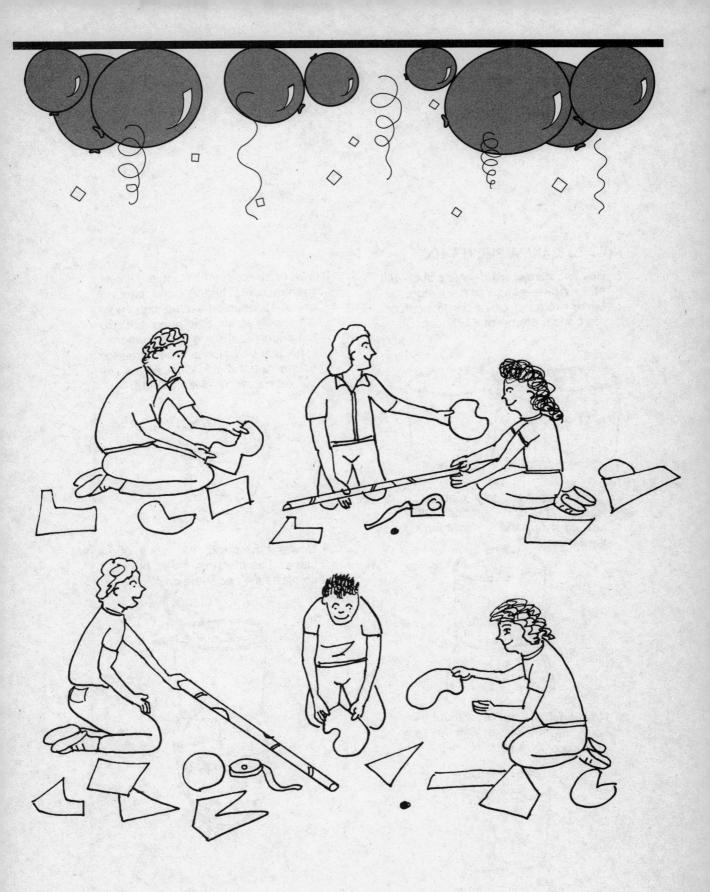

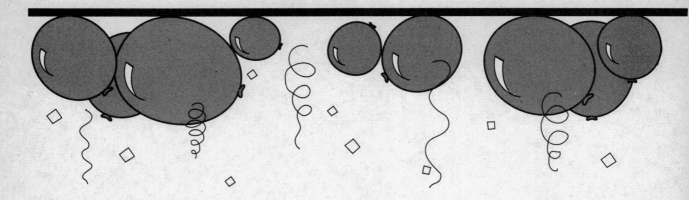

HOW TO MAKE A BUCKET HAT

1. Buy two cardboard painter's buckets at a hardware store or paint store. Make two holes on opposite sides of the bottom of one of the buckets.

2. Take a 3-foot length of clothesline or waistband elastic (purchased at a sewing shop) and thread it through the holes.

3. Now, push the bucket without the holes into the bucket with the strap until it's a snug fit.

4. Before strapping the double buckets to the players' heads, have them put on an adjustable baseball cap that fits snugly around the head, but not too snugly to the top of the head. (The little bit of loose area at the top acts as a soft foundation, so the bucket hat won't slide around.)

5. Now put the bucket hat on top of the cap and tie the strap firmly, but comfortably, under the chin.

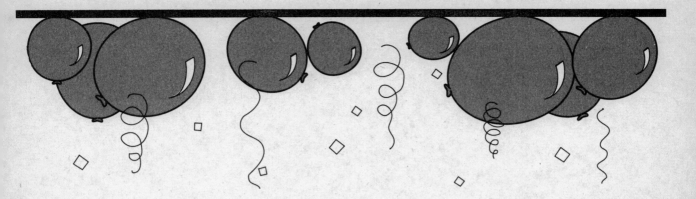

HOW TO MAKE A CONTAINER HAT

1. Buy 2 plastic quart-sized deli or freezer containers. On opposite sides of the bottom of one of the containers, make 2 holes big enough for a length of clothesline or waistband elastic to pass through. (Buy elastic at a sewing shop.)

2. Pass a 3-foot piece of rope or elastic material through the holes.

3. Push the container without the holes into the first container (with the strap) so it's a snug fit.

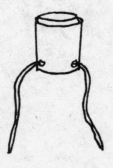

4. Before strapping the doubled containers onto the players' heads, have them put on an adjustable baseball cap that fits snugly around the head, but not too snugly to the top of the head. (This little bit of looseness at the top acts as a soft foundation, so the container hat won't slide around.)

5. Now, place the double container hat on top of the cap and tie the strap firmly, but comfortably, under the chin.

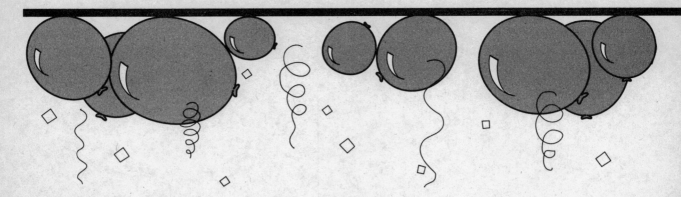

HOW TO MAKE A TRAY HAT AND A FLAT TOP HAT

1. From a liquor or grocery store, get a cardboard soda can tray. Make 2 holes on the bottom, one each at the farthest edges on opposite sides of the tray.

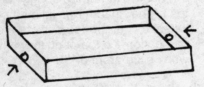

2. Thread a 3-foot long piece of clothesline or waistband elastic through the holes.

3. Place the tray on top of an adjustable baseball cap that fits snugly around the head, but not too snugly on top of the head. (This bit of looseness on top acts as a soft foundation, so the tray won't slide around.)

4. Tie the tray strap firmly but comfortably under the chin. Note: You can use the tray hat for the flat-top hat. All you have to do is turn the tray upside down, so the edge of the tray is facing down.

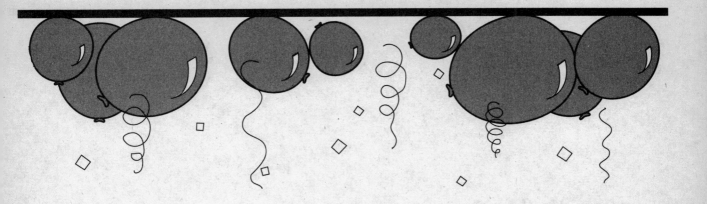

Games Using the Same Materials

This list gives you the opportunity to play several games using the same materials or objects to cut down on your cost and preparation time.

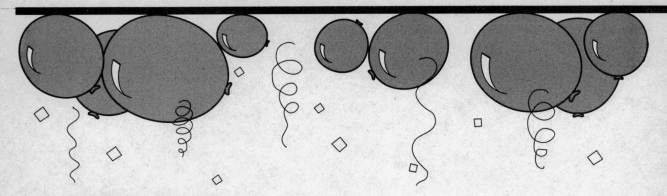

Send Us Your Games

Have you invented a party game for kids 8 to 15 years old—that's messy, clean, zany, brainy, or just plain fun using mostly household items? How about a wacky snack, unusual invitations, crazy cakes, or special birthday surprises? Send them to me, and maybe we'll include them in a future edition. (Please do not send anything you need returned.)

Mail them to: Tracy Stephen Burroughs
P.O. Box 785
Georgetown, CT 06829